Thomas Win
Curate V1

George MacDonald

Alpha Editions

This edition published in 2023

ISBN : 9789357944731

Design and Setting By
Alpha Editions
www.alphaedis.com
Email - info@alphaedis.com

Contents

VOL I.

CHAPTER I.
HELEN LINGARD.

A swift, gray November wind had taken every chimney of the house for an organ-pipe, and was roaring in them all at once, quelling the more distant and varied noises of the woods, which moaned and surged like a sea. Helen Lingard had not been out all day. The morning, indeed, had been fine, but she had been writing a long letter to her brother Leopold at Cambridge, and had put off her walk in the neighbouring park till after luncheon, and in the meantime the wind had risen, and brought with it a haze that threatened rain. She was in admirable health, had never had a day's illness in her life, was hardly more afraid of getting wet than a young farmer, and enjoyed wind, especially when she was on horseback. Yet as she stood looking from her window, across a balcony where shivered more than one autumnal plant that ought to have been removed a week ago, out upon the old-fashioned garden and meadows beyond, where each lonely tree bowed with drifting garments—I was going to say, like a suppliant, but it was AWAY from its storming enemy—she did not feel inclined to go out. That she was healthy was no reason why she should be unimpressible, any more than that good temper should be a reason for indifference to the behaviour of one's friend. She always felt happier in a new dress, when it was made to her mind and fitted her body; and when the sun shone she was lighter-hearted than when it rained: I had written MERRIER, but Helen was seldom merry, and had she been made aware of the fact, and questioned why, would have answered—Because she so seldom saw reason.

She was what all her friends called a sensible girl; but, as I say, that was no reason why she should be an insensible girl as well, and be subject to none of the influences of the weather. She did feel those influences, and therefore it was that she turned away from the window with the sense, rather than the conviction, that the fireside in her own room was rendered even, more attractive by the unfriendly aspect of things outside and the roar in the chimney, which happily was not accompanied by a change in the current of the smoke.

The hours between luncheon and tea are confessedly dull, but dulness is not inimical to a certain kind of comfort, and Helen liked to be that way comfortable. Nor had she ever yet been aware of self-rebuke because of the liking. Let us see what kind and degree of comfort she had in the course of an hour and a half attained. And in discovering this I shall be able to present her to my reader with a little more circumstance.

She sat before the fire in a rather masculine posture. I would not willingly be rude, but the fact remains—a posture in which she would not, I think, have sat for her photograph—leaning back in a chintz-covered easy-chair, all the lines of direction about her parallel with the lines of the chair, her arms lying on its arms, and the fingers of each hand folded down over the end of each arm—square, straight, right-angled,—gazing into the fire, with something of the look of a sage, but one who has made no discovery.

She had just finished the novel of the day, and was suffering a mild reaction—the milder, perhaps, that she was not altogether satisfied with the consummation. For the heroine had, after much sorrow and patient endurance, at length married a man whom she could not help knowing to be not worth having. For the author even knew it, only such was his reading of life, and such his theory of artistic duty, that what it was a disappointment to Helen to peruse, it seemed to have been a comfort to him to write. Indeed, her dissatisfaction went so far that, although the fire kept burning away in perfect content before her, enhanced by the bellowing complaint of the wind in the chimney, she yet came nearer thinking than she had ever been in her life. Now thinking, especially to one who tries it for the first time, is seldom, or never, a quite comfortable operation, and hence Helen was very near becoming actually uncomfortable. She was even on the borders of making the unpleasant discovery that the business of life—and that not only for North Pole expeditions, African explorers, pyramid-inspectors, and such like, but for every man and woman born into the blindness of the planet—is to discover; after which discovery there is little more comfort to be had of the sort with which Helen was chiefly conversant. But she escaped for the time after a very simple and primitive fashion, although it was indeed a narrow escape.

Let me not be misunderstood, however, and supposed to imply that Helen was dull in faculty, or that she contributed nothing to the bubbling of the intellectual pool in the social gatherings at Glaston. Far from it. When I say that she came near thinking, I say more for her than any but the few who know what thinking is will understand, for that which chiefly distinguishes man from those he calls the lower animals is the faculty he most rarely exercises. True, Helen supposed she could think—like other people, because the thoughts of other people had passed through her in tolerable plenty, leaving many a phantom conclusion behind; but this was THEIR thinking, not hers. She had thought no more than was necessary now and then to the persuasion that she saw what a sentence meant, after which, her acceptance or rejection of what was contained in it, never more than lukewarm, depended solely upon its relation to what she had somehow or other, she could seldom have told how, come to regard as the proper style of opinion to hold upon things in general.

The social matrix which up to this time had ministered to her development, had some relations with Mayfair, it is true, but scanty ones indeed with the universe; so that her present condition was like that of the common bees, every one of which Nature fits for a queen, but its nurses, prevent from growing one by providing for it a cell too narrow for the unrolling of royalty, and supplying it with food not potent enough for the nurture of the ideal— with this difference, however, that the cramped and stinted thing comes out, if no queen, then a working bee, and Helen, who might be both, was neither yet. If I were at liberty to mention the books on her table, it would give a few of my readers no small help towards the settling of her position in the "valued file" of the young women of her generation; but there are reasons against it.

She was the daughter of an officer, who, her mother dying when she was born, committed her to the care of a widowed aunt, and almost immediately left for India, where he rose to high rank, and somehow or other amassed a considerable fortune, partly through his marriage with a Hindoo lady, by whom he had one child, a boy some three years younger than Helen. When he died, he left his fortune equally divided between the two children.

Helen was now three-and-twenty, and her own mistress. Her appearance suggested Norwegian blood, for she was tall, blue-eyed, and dark-haired— but fair-skinned, with regular features, and an over still-some who did not like her said hard—expression of countenance. No one had ever called her NELLY; yet she had long remained a girl, lingering on the broken borderland after several of her school companions had become young matrons. Her drawing-master, a man of some observation and insight, used to say Miss Lingard would wake up somewhere about forty.

The cause of her so nearly touching the borders of thought this afternoon, was, that she became suddenly aware of feeling bored. Now Helen was even seldomer bored than merry, and this time she saw no reason for it, neither had any person to lay the blame upon. She might have said it was the weather, but the weather had never done it before. Nor could it be want of society, for George Bascombe was to dine with them. So was the curate, but he did not count for much. Neither was she weary of herself. That, indeed, might be only a question of time, for the most complete egotist, Julius Caesar, or Napoleon Bonaparte, must at length get weary of his paltry self; but Helen, from the slow rate of her expansion, was not old enough yet. Nor was she in any special sense wrapt up in herself: it was only that she had never yet broken the shell which continues to shut in so many human chickens, long after they imagine themselves citizens of the real world.

Being somewhat bored then, and dimly aware that to be bored was out of harmony with something or other, Helen was on the verge of thinking, but, as I have said, escaped the snare in a very direct and simple fashion: she went

fast asleep, and never woke till her maid brought her the cup of kitchen-tea from which the inmates of some houses derive the strength to prepare for dinner.

CHAPTER II.

THOMAS WINGFOLD.

The morning, whose afternoon was thus stormy, had been fine, and the curate went out for a walk. Had it been just as stormy, however, he would have gone all the same. Not that he was a great walker, or, indeed, fond of exercise of any sort, and his walking, as an Irishman might say, was half sitting—on stiles and stones and fallen trees. He was not in bad health, he was not lazy, or given to self-preservation, but he had little impulse to activity of any sort. The springs in his well of life did not seem to flow quite fast enough.

He strolled through Osterfield park, and down the deep descent to the river, where, chilly as it was, he seated himself upon a large stone on the bank, and knew that he was there, and that he had to answer to Thomas Wingfold; but why he was there, and why he was not called something else, he did not know. On each side of the stream rose a steeply-sloping bank, on which grew many fern-bushes, now half withered, and the sunlight upon them, this November morning, seemed as cold as the wind that blew about their golden and green fronds. Over a rocky bottom the stream went—talking rather than singing—down the valley towards the town, where it seemed to linger a moment to embrace the old abbey church, before it set out on its leisurely slide through the low level to the sea. Its talk was chilly, and its ripples, which came half from the obstructions in its channel below, and half from the wind that ruffled it above, were not smiles, but wrinkles rather—even in the sunshine. Thomas felt cold himself, but the cold was of the sort that comes from the look rather than the feel of things. He did not, however, much care how he felt—not enough, certainly, to have made him put on a great-coat: he was not deeply interested in himself. With his stick, a very ordinary bit of oak, he kept knocking pebbles into the water, and listlessly watching them splash. The wind blew, the sun shone, the water ran, the ferns waved, the clouds went drifting over his head, but he never looked up, or took any notice of the doings of Mother Nature at her house-work: everything seemed to him to be doing only what it had got to do, because it had got it to do, and not because it cared about it, or had any end in doing it. For he, like every other man, could read nature only by his own lamp, and this was very much how he had hitherto responded to the demands made upon him.

His life had not been a very interesting one, although early passages in it had been painful. He had done fairly well at Oxford: it had been expected of him, and he had answered expectation; he had not distinguished himself, nor cared to do so. He had known from the first that he was intended for the church, and had not objected, but received it as his destiny—had even, in dim obedience, kept before his mental vision the necessity of yielding to the heights and hollows of the mould into which he was being thrust. But he had taken no great interest in the matter.

The church was to him an ancient institution of such approved respectability that it was able to communicate it, possessing emoluments, and requiring observances. He had entered her service; she was his mistress, and in return for the narrow shelter, humble fare, and not quite too shabby garments she allotted him, he would perform her hests—in the spirit of a servant who abideth not in the house for ever. He was now six and twenty years of age, and had never dreamed of marriage, or even been troubled with a thought of its unattainable remoteness. He did not philosophize much upon life or his position in it, taking everything with a cold, hopeless kind of acceptance, and laying no claim to courage, devotion, or even bare suffering. He had a certain dull prejudice in favour of honesty, would not have told the shadow of a lie to be made Archbishop of Canterbury, and yet was so uninstructed in the things that constitute practical honesty that some of his opinions would have considerably astonished St. Paul. He liked reading the prayers, for the making of them vocal in the church was pleasant to him, and he had a not unmusical voice. He visited the sick—with some repugnance, it is true, but without delay, and spoke to them such religious commonplaces as occurred to him, depending mainly on the prayers belonging to their condition for the right performance of his office. He never thought about being a gentleman, but always behaved like one.

I suspect that at this time there lay somewhere in his mind, keeping generally well out of sight however, that is, below the skin of his consciousness, the unacknowledged feeling that he had been hardly dealt with. But at no time, even when it rose plainest, would he have dared to add—by Providence. Had the temptation come, he would have banished it and the feeling together.

He did not read much, browsed over his newspaper at breakfast with a polite curiosity, sufficient to season the loneliness of his slice of fried bacon, and took more interest in some of the naval intelligence than in anything else. Indeed it would have been difficult for himself even to say in what he did take a large interest. When leisure awoke a question as to how he should employ it, he would generally take up his Horace and read aloud one of his more mournful odes—with such attention to the rhythm, I must add, as, although plentiful enough among scholars in respect of the dead letter, is rarely found with them in respect of the living vocal utterance.

Nor had he now sat long upon his stone, heedless of the world's preparations for winter, before he began repeating to himself the poet's Æquam memento rebus in arduis, which he had been trying much, but with small success, to reproduce in similar English cadences, moved thereto in part by the success of Tennyson in his O mighty-mouthed inventor of harmonies—a thing as yet alone in the language, so far as I know. It was perhaps a little strange that the curate should draw the strength of which he was most conscious from the pages of a poet whose hereafter was chiefly servicable to him— in virtue of its unsubstantiality and poverty, the dreamlike thinness of its reality—in enhancing the pleasures of the world of sun and air, cooling shade and songful streams, the world of wine and jest, of forms that melted more slowly from encircling arms, and eyes that did not so swiftly fade and vanish in the distance. Yet when one reflects but for a moment on the poverty-stricken expectations of Christians from their hereafter, I cease to wonder at Wingfold; for human sympathy is lovely and pleasant, and if a Christian priest and a pagan poet feel much in the same tone concerning the affairs of a universe, why should they not comfort each other by sitting down together in the dust?

"No hair it boots thee whether from Inachus
  Ancient descended, or, of the poorest born,
    Thy being drags, all bare and roofless—
      Victim the same to the heartless Orcus.

All are on one road driven; for each of us
  The urn is tossed, and, later or earlier,
    The lot will drop and all be sentenced
      Into the boat of eternal exile."

Having thus far succeeded with these two stanzas, Wingfold rose, a little pleased with himself, and climbed the bank above him, wading through mingled sun and wind and ferns—so careless of their shivering beauty and their coming exile, that a watcher might have said the prospect of one day leaving behind him the shows of this upper world could have no part in the curate's sympathy with Horace.

CHAPTER III.

THE DINERS.

Mrs. Ramshorn, Helen's aunt, was past the middle age of woman; had been handsome and pleasing, had long ceased to be either; had but sparingly recognised the fact, yet had recognised it, and felt aggrieved. Hence in part it was that her mouth had gathered that peevish and wronged expression which tends to produce a moral nausea in the beholder. If she had but known how much uglier in the eyes of her fellow mortals her own discontent made her, than the severest operation of the laws of mortal decay could have done, she might have tried to think less of her wrongs and more of her privileges. As it was, her own face wronged her own heart, which was still womanly, and capable of much pity—seldom exercised. Her husband had been dean of Halystone, a man of insufficient weight of character to have the right influence in the formation of his wife's. He had left her tolerably comfortable as to circumstances, but childless. She loved Helen, whose even imperturbability had by mere weight, as it might seem, gained such a power over her that she was really mistress in the house without either of them knowing it.

Naturally desirous of keeping Helen's fortune in the family, and having, as I say, no son of her own, she had yet not far to look to find a cousin capable, as she might well imagine, of rendering himself acceptable to the heiress. He was the son of her younger sister, married, like herself, to a dignitary of the Church, a canon of a northern cathedral. This youth, therefore, Greorge Bascombe by name, whose visible calling at present was to eat his way to the bar, she often invited to Glaston; and on this Friday afternoon he was on his way from London to spend the Saturday and Sunday with the two ladies. The cousins liked each other, had not had more of each other's society than was favourable to their aunt's designs, who was far too prudent to have made as yet any reference to them, and stood altogether in as suitable a relative position for falling in love with each other as Mrs. Ramshorn could well have desired. Her chief, almost her only uneasiness, arose from the important and but too evident fact, that Helen Lingard was not a girl of the sort to fall readily in love. That, however, was of no consequence, provided it did not come in the way of marrying her cousin, who, her aunt felt confident, was better fitted to rouse her dormant affections than any other youth she had ever seen, or was ever likely to see. Upon this occasion she had asked Thomas Wingfold to meet him, partly with the design that he should act as a foil to her nephew, partly in order to do her duty by the church, to which she felt herself belong not as a lay member, but in some undefined professional capacity, in virtue of her departed dean. Wingfold had but lately come to the parish, and, as he was merely curate, she had not been in haste to invite him.

On the other hand, he was the only clergyman officiating in the abbey church, which was grand and old, with a miserable living and a non-resident rector. He, to do him justice, paid nearly the amount of the tithes in salary to his curate, and spent the rest on the church material, of which, for certain reasons, he retained the incumbency, the presentation to which belonged to his own family.

The curate presented himself at the dinner-hour in Mrs. Ramshorn's drawing-room, looking like any other gentleman, satisfied with his share in the administration of things, and affecting nothing of the professional either in dress, manner, or tone. Helen saw him for the first time in private life, and, as she had expected, saw nothing remarkable—a man who looked about thirty, was a little over the middle height, and well enough constructed as men go, had a good forehead, a questionable nose, clear grey eyes, long, mobile, sensitive mouth, large chin, pale complexion, and straight black hair, and might have been a lawyer just as well as a clergyman. A keener, that is, a more interested eye than hers, might have discovered traces of suffering in the forms of the wrinkles which, as he talked, would now and then flit like ripples over his forehead; but Helen's eyes seldom did more than slip over the faces presented to her; and had it been otherwise, who could be expected to pay much regard to Thomas Wingfold when George Bascombe was present? There, indeed, stood a man by the corner of the mantelpiece!—tall and handsome as an Apollo, and strong as the young Hercules, dressed in the top of the plainest fashion, self-satisfied, but not offensively so, good-natured, ready to smile, as clean in conscience, apparently, and as large in sympathy, as his shirt-front. Everybody who knew him, counted George Bascombe a genuine good fellow, and George himself knew little to the contrary, while Helen knew nothing.

One who had only chanced to get a glimpse of her in her own room, as in imagination my reader has done, would hardly have recognised her again in the drawing-room. For in her own room she was but as she appeared to herself in her mirror—dull, inanimate; but in the drawing-room her reflection from living eyes and presences served to stir up what waking life was in her. When she spoke, her face dawned with a clear, although not warm light; and although it must be owned that when it was at rest, the same over-stillness, amounting almost to dulness, the same seeming immobility, ruled as before, yet, even when she was not speaking, the rest was often broken by a smile—a genuine one, for although there was much that was stiff, there was nothing artificial about Helen. Neither was there much of the artificial about her cousin; for his good-nature, and his smile, and whatever else appeared upon him, were all genuine enough—the only thing in this respect not quite satisfactory to the morally fastidious man being his tone in speaking. Whether he had caught it at the university, or amongst his father's clerical friends, or in the professional society he now frequented, I cannot tell, but it had been manufactured somewhere—after a large, scrolly kind of pattern, sounding well-bred and dignified. I wonder how many speak with the voices that really belong to them.

Plainly, to judge from the one Bascombe used, he was accustomed to lay down the law, but in gentlemanly fashion, and not as if he cared a bit about the thing in question himself. By the side of his easy carriage, his broad chest, and towering Greek-shaped head, Thomas Wingfold dwindled almost to vanishing—in a word, looked nobody. And besides his inferiority in size and self-presentment, he had a slight hesitation of manner, which seemed to anticipate, if not to court, the subordinate position which most men, and most women too, were ready to assign him. He said, "Don't you think?" far oftener than "I think" and was always more ready to fix his attention upon the strong points of an opponent's argument than to re-assert his own in slightly altered phrase like most men, or even in fresh forms like a few; hence—self-assertion, either modestly worn like a shirt of fine chain-armour, or gaunt and obtrusive like plates of steel, being the strength of the ordinary man—what could the curate appear but defenceless, therefore weak, and therefore contemptible? The truth is, he had less self-conceit than a mortal's usual share, and was not yet possessed of any opinions interesting enough to himself to seem worth defending with any approach to vivacity.

Bascombe and he bowed in response to their introduction with proper indifference, after a moment's solemn pause exchanged a sentence or two which resembled an exercise in the proper use of a foreign language, and then gave what attention Englishmen are capable of before dinner to the two ladies—the elder of whom, I may just mention, was dressed in black velvet with heavy Venetian lace, and the younger in black silk, with old Honiton. Neither of them did much towards enlivening the conversation. Mrs. Ramshorn, whose dinner had as yet gained in interest with her years, sat peevishly longing for its arrival, but cast every now and then a look of mild satisfaction upon her nephew, which, however, while it made her eyes sweeter, did not much alter the expression of her mouth. Helen improved, as she fancied, the arrangement of a few green-house flowers in an ugly vase on the table.

At length the butler appeared, the curate took Mrs. Ramshorn, and the cousins followed—making, in the judgment of the butler as he stood in the hall, and the housekeeper as she peeped from the baise-covered door that led to the still-room, as handsome a couple as mortal eyes need wish to see. They looked nearly of an age, the lady the more stately, the gentleman the more graceful, or, perhaps rather, ELEGANT, of the two.

CHAPTER IV.

THEIR TALK.

During dinner, Bascombe had the talk mostly to himself, and rattled well, occasionally rebuked by his aunt for some remark which might to a clergyman appear objectionable; nor as a partisan was she altogether satisfied with the curate that he did not seem inclined to take clerical exception. He ate his dinner, quietly responding to Bascombe's sallies—which had usually more of vivacity than keenness, more of good spirits than wit—with a curious flickering smile, or a single word of agreement. It might have seemed that he was humouring a younger man, but the truth was, the curate had not yet seen cause for opposing him.

How any friend could have come to send Helen poetry I cannot imagine, but that very morning she had received by post a small volume of verse, which, although just out, and by an unknown author, had already been talked of in what are called literary circles. Wingfold had read some extracts from the book that same morning, and was therefore not quite unprepared when Helen asked him if he had seen it. He suggested that the poems, if the few lines he had seen made a fair sample, were rather of the wailful order.

"If there is one thing I despise more than another," said Bascombe, "it is to hear a man, a fellow with legs and arms, pour out his griefs into the bosom of that most discreet of confidantes, Society, bewailing his hard fate, and calling upon youths and maidens to fill their watering-pots with tears, and with him water the sorrowful pansies and undying rue of the race. I believe I am quoting."

"I think you must be, George," said Helen. "I never knew you venture so near the edge of poetry before."

"Ah, that is all you know of me, Miss Lingard!" returned Bascombe. "—And then," he resumed, turning again to Wingfold, "what is it they complain of? That some girls preferred a better man perhaps, or that a penny paper once told the truth of their poetry."

"Or it may be only that it is their humour to be sad," said Wingfold. "But don't you think," he continued, "it is hardly worth while to be indignant with them? Their verses are a relief to them, and do nobody any harm."

"They do all the boys and girls harm that read them, and themselves who write them more harm than anybody, confirming them in tearful habits, and teaching eyes unused to weep. I quote again, I believe, but from whom I am innocent. If I ever had a grief, I should have along with it the decency to keep it to myself."

"I don't doubt you would, George," said his cousin, who seemed more playfully inclined than usual. "But," she added, with a smile, "would your silence be voluntary, or enforced?"

"What!" returned Bascombe, "you think I could not plain my woes to the moon? Why not I as well as another? I could roar you as 'twere any nightingale."

"You have had your sorrows, then, George?"

"Never anything worse yet than a tailor's bill, Helen, and I hope you won't provide me with any. I am not in love with decay. I remember a fellow at Trinity, the merriest of all our set at a wine-party, who, alone with his ink-pot, was for ever enacting the part of the unheeded poet, complaining of the hard hearts and tuneless ears of his generation. I went into his room once, and found him with the tears running down his face, a pot of stout half empty on the table, and his den all but opaque with tobacco-smoke, reciting, with sobs—I had repeated the lines so often before they ceased to amuse me, that I can never forget them—

'Heard'st thou a quiver and clang?
    In thy sleep did it make thee start?
  'Twas a chord in twain that sprang—
    But the lyre-shell was my heart.'

He took a pull at the stout, laid his head on the table, and sobbed like a locomotive."

"But it's not very bad—not bad at all, so far as I see," said Helen, who had a woman's weakness for the side attacked, in addition to a human partiality for fair play.

"No, not bad at all—for absolute nonsense," said Bascombe.

"He had been reading Heine," said Wingfold.

"And burlesquing him," returned Bascombe. "Fancy hearing one of the fellow's heart-strings crack, and taking it for a string of his fiddle in the press! By the way, what are the heart-strings? Have they any anatomical synonym? But I have no doubt it was good poetry."

"Do you think poetry and common sense necessarily opposed to each other?" asked Wingfold.

"I confess a leaning to that opinion," replied Bascombe, with a half-conscious smile.

"What do you say of Horace, now?" suggested Wingfold.

"Unfortunately for me, you have mentioned the one poet for whom I have any respect. But what I like in him is just his common sense. He never cries over spilt milk, even if the jug be broken to the bargain. But common sense would be just as good in prose as in verse."

"Possibly; but what we have of it in Horace would never have reached us but for the forms into which he has cast it. How much more enticing acorns in the cup are! I was watching two children picking them up to-day."

"That may be; there have always been more children than grown men," returned Bascombe. "For my part, I would sweep away all illusions, and get at the heart of the affair."

"But," said Wingfold, with the look of one who, as he tries to say it, is seeing a thing for the first time, "does not the acorn-cup belong to the acorn? May not some of what you call illusions, be the finer, or at least more ethereal qualities of the thing itself? You do not object to music in church, for instance?"

Bascombe was on the point of saying he objected to it nowhere except in church, but for his aunt's sake, or rather for his own sake in his aunt's eyes, he restrained himself, and uttered his feelings only in a peculiar smile, of import so mingled, that its meaning was illegible ere it had quivered along his lip and vanished.

"I am no metaphysician," he said, and Wingfold accepted the dismissal of the subject.

Little passed between the two men over their wine; and as neither of them cared to drink more than a couple of glasses, they soon rejoined the ladies in the drawing-room.

Mrs. Ramshorn was taking her usual forty winks in her arm-chair, and their entrance did not disturb her. Helen was turning over some music.

"I am looking for a song for you, George," she said. "I want Mr. Wingfold to hear you sing, lest he should take you for a man of stone and lime."

"Never mind looking," returned her cousin. "I will sing one you have never heard."

And seating himself at the piano, he sang the following verses. They were his own, a fact he would probably have allowed to creep out, had they met with more sympathy. His voice was a full bass one, full of tone.

"Each man has his lampful, his lampful of oil;
  He may dull its glimmer with sorrow and toil;
  He may leave it unlit, and let it dry,
  Or wave it aloft, and hold it high:

For mine, it shall burn with a fearless flame
In the front of the darkness that has no name.

"Sunshine and Wind?—are ye there? Ho! ho!
Are ye comrades or lords, as ye shine and blow?
I care not, I! I will lift my head
Till ye shine and blow on my grassy bed.
See, brother Sun, I am shining too!
Wind, I am living as well as you!

"Though the sun go out like a vagrant spark,
And his daughter planets are left in the dark,
I care not, I! For why should I care?
I shall be hurtless, nor here nor there.
Sun and Wind, let us shine and shout,
For the day draws nigh when we all go out!"

"I don't like the song," said Helen, wrinkling her brows a little. "It sounds—well, heathenish."

She would, I fear, have said nothing of the sort, being used to that kind of sound from her cousin, had not a clergyman been present. Yet she said it from no hypocrisy, but simple regard to his professional feelings,

"I sung it for Mr. Wingfold," returned Bascombe. "It would have been a song after Horace's own heart."

"Don't you think," rejoined the curate, "the defiant tone of your song would have been strange to him? I confess that what I find chiefly attractive in Horace is his sad submission to the inevitable."

"Sad?" echoed Bascombe.

"Don't you think so?"

"No. He makes the best of it, and as merrily as he can."

"AS HE CAN, I grant you," said Wingfold.

Here Mrs. Ramshorn woke, and the subject was dropped, leaving Mr. Wingfold in some perplexity as to this young man and his talk, and what the phenomenon signified. Was heathenism after all secretly cherished, and about to become fashionable in English society? He saw little of its phases, and for what he knew it might be so.

Helen sat down to the piano. Her time was perfect, and she never blundered a note. She played well and woodenly, and had for her reward a certain wooden satisfaction in her own performance. The music she chose was good of its kind, but had more to do with the instrument than the feelings, and was more dependent upon execution than expression. Bascombe yawned behind his handkerchief, and Wingfold gazed at the profile of the player, wondering how, with such fine features and complexion, with such a fine-shaped and well-set head? her face should be so far short of interesting. It seemed a face that had no story.

CHAPTER V.

A STAGGERING QUESTION.

It was time the curate should take his leave. Bascombe would go out with him and have his last cigar. The wind had fallen, and the moon was shining. A vague sense of contrast came over Wingfold, and as he stepped on the pavement from the threshold of the high gates of wrought iron, he turned involuntarily and looked back at the house. It was of red brick, and flat-faced in the style of Queen Anne's time, so that the light could do nothing with it in the way of shadow, and dwelt only on the dignity of its unpretentiousness. But aloft over its ridge the moon floated in the softest, loveliest blue, with just a cloud here and there to show how blue it was, and a sparkle where its blueness took fire in a star. It was autumn, almost winter, below, and the creepers that clung to the house waved in the now gentle wind like the straggling tresses of old age; but above was a sky that might have overhung the last melting of spring into summer. At the end of the street rose the great square tower of the church, seeming larger than in the daylight. There was something in it all that made the curate feel there ought to be more—as if the night knew something he did not; and he yielded himself to its invasion.

His companion having carefully lighted his cigar all round its extreme periphery, took it from his mouth, regarded its glowing end with a smile of satisfaction, and burst into a laugh. It was not a scornful laugh, neither was it a merry or a humorous laugh; it was one of satisfaction and amusement.

"Let me have a share in the fun," said the curate.

"You have it," said his companion—rudely, indeed, but not quite offensively, and put his cigar in his mouth again.

Wingfold was not one to take umbrage easily. He was not important enough in his own eyes for that, but he did not choose to go farther.

"That's a fine old church," he said, pointing to the dark mass invading the blue—so solid, yet so clear in outline.

"I am glad the mason-work is to your mind," returned Bascombe, almost compassionately. "It must be some satisfaction, perhaps consolation to you."

Before he had thus concluded the sentence a little scorn had crept into his tone.

"You make some allusion which I do not quite apprehend," said the curate.

"Now, I am going to be honest with you," said Bascombe abruptly, and stopping, he turned towards his companion, and took the full-flavoured Havannah from his lips. "I like you," he went on, "for you seem reasonable;

and besides, a man ought to speak out what he thinks. So here goes!—Tell me honestly—do you believe one word of all that!"

And he in his turn pointed in the direction of the great tower.

The curate was taken by surprise and made no answer: it was as if he had received a sudden blow in the face. Recovering himself presently, however, he sought room to pass the question without direct encounter.

"How came the thing there?" he said, once more indicating the church-tower.

"By faith, no doubt," answered Bascombe, laughing,—"but not your faith; no, nor the faith of any of the last few generations."

"There are more churches built now, ten times over, than in any former period of our history."

"True; but of what sort? All imitation—never an original amongst them all!"

"If they had found out the right way, why change it?"

"Good! But it is rather ominous for the claim of a divine origin to your religion that it should be the only one thing that in these days takes the crab's move—backwards. You are indebted to your forefathers for your would-be belief, as well as for their genuine churches. You hardly know what your belief is. There is my aunt—as good a specimen as I know of what you call a Christian!—so accustomed is she to think and speak too after the forms of what you heard my cousin call heathenism, that she would never have discovered, had she been as wide awake as she was sound asleep, that the song I sung was anything but a good Christian ballad."

"Pardon me; I think you are wrong there."

"What! did you never remark how these Christian people, who profess to believe that their great man has conquered death, and all that rubbish—did you never observe the way they look if the least allusion is made to death, or the eternity they say they expect beyond it? Do they not stare as if you had committed a breach of manners? Religion itself is the same way: as much as you like about the church, but don't mention Christ! At the same time, to do them justice, it is only of death in the abstract they decline to hear; they will listen to the news of the death of a great and good man, without any such emotion. Look at the poetry of death—I mean the way Christian poets write of it! A dreamless sleep they call it—the bourne from whence, knows no waking. 'She is gone for ever!' cries the mother over her daughter. And that is why such things are not to be mentioned, because in their hearts they have no hope, and in their minds no courage to face the facts of existence. We haven't the pluck of the old fellows, who, that they might look death himself in the face without dismay, accustomed themselves, even at their banquets, to the sight of his most loathsome handiwork, his most significant symbol—and enjoyed their wine the better for it!—your friend Horace, for instance."

"But your aunt now would never consent to such an interpretation of her opinions. Nor do I allow that it is fair."

"My dear sir, if there is one thing I pride myself upon, it is fair play, and I grant you at once she would not. But I am speaking, not of creeds, but of beliefs. And I assert that the forms of common Christian speech regarding death come nearer those of Horace than your saint, the old Jew, Saul of Tarsus."

It did not occur to Wingfold that people generally speak from the surfaces, not the depths of their minds, even when those depths are moved; nor yet that possibly Mrs. Ramshorn was not the best type of a Christian, even in his soft-walking congregation! In fact, nothing came into his mind with which to meet what Bascombe said—the real force whereof he could not help feeling—and he answered nothing. His companion followed his apparent yielding with fresh pressure.

"In truth," he said, "I do not believe that YOU believe more than an atom here and there of what you profess. I am confident you have more good sense by a great deal."

"I am sorry to find that you place good sense above good faith, Mr. Bascombe; but I am obliged by your good opinion, which, as I read it, amounts to this—that I am one of the greatest humbugs you have the misfortune to be acquainted with."

"Ha! ha! ha!—No, no; I don't say that. I know so well how to make allowance for the prejudices a man has inherited from foolish ancestors, and which have been instilled into him, as well, with his earliest nourishment, both bodily and mental. But—come now—I do love open dealing—I am myself open as the day—did you not take to the church as a profession, in which you might eat a piece of bread—as somebody says in your own blessed Bible—dry enough bread it may be, for the old lady is not over-generous to her younger children—still a gentlemanly sort of livelihood?"

Wingfold held his peace. It was incontestably with such a view that he had signed the articles and sought holy orders—and that without a single question as to truth or reality in either act.

"Your silence is honesty, Mr. Wingfold, and I honour you for it," said Bascombe. "It is an easy thing for a man in another profession to speak his mind, but silence such as yours, casting a shadow backward over your past, require courage: I honour you, sir."

As he spoke, he laid his hand on Wingfold's shoulder with the grasp of an athlete.

"Can the sherry have anything to do with it?" thought the curate. The fellow was, or seemed to be, years younger than himself! It was an assurance unimaginable—yet there it stood—six feet of it good! He glanced at the church tower. It had not vanished in mist! It still made its own strong, clear mark on the eternal blue!

"I must not allow you to mistake my silence, Mr. Bascombe," he answered the same moment. "It is not easy to reply to such demands all at once. It is not easy to say in times like these, and at a moment's notice, what or how much a man believes. But whatever my answer might be had I time to consider it, my silence must at least not be interpreted to mean that I do NOT believe as my profession indicates. That, at all events, would be untrue."

"Then I am to understand, Mr. Wingfold, that you neither believe nor disbelieve the tenets of the church whose bread you eat?" said Bascombe, with the air of a reprover of sin.

"I decline to place myself between the horns of any such dilemma," returned Wingfold, who was now more than a little annoyed at his persistency in forcing his way within the precincts of another's personality.

"It is but one more proof—more than was necessary—to convince me that the old system is a lie—a lie of the worst sort, seeing it may prevail even to the self-deception of a man otherwise remarkable for honesty and directness. Good night, Mr. Wingfold."

With lifted hats, but no hand-shaking, the men parted.

CHAPTER VI.

THE CURATE IN THE CHURCHYARD.

Bascombe was chagrined to find that the persuasive eloquence with which he hoped soon to play upon the convictions of jurymen at his own sweet will, had not begotten even communicativenes, not to say confidence, in the mind of a parson who knew himself fooled,—and partly that it gave him cause to doubt how far it might be safe to urge his attack in another and to him more important quarter. He had a passion for convincing people, this Hercules of the new world. He sauntered slowly back to his aunt's, husbanding his cigar a little, and looking up at the moon now and then,—not to admire the marvel of her shining, but to think yet again what a fit type of an effete superstition she was, in that she retained her power of fascination even in death.

Wingfold walked slowly away, with his eyes on the ground gliding from under his footsteps. It was only eleven o'clock, but this the oldest part of the town seemed already asleep. They had not met a single person on their way, and hardly seen a lighted window. But he felt unwilling to go home, which at first he was fain to attribute to his having drunk a little more wine than was good for him, whence this feverishness and restlessness so strange to his experience. In the churchyard, on the other side of which his lodging lay, he turned aside from the flagged path and sat down upon a gravestone, where he was hardly seated ere he began to discover that it was something else than the wine which had made him feel so uncomfortable. What an objectionable young fellow that Bascombe was! —presuming and arrogant to a degree rare, he hoped, even in a profession for which insolence was a qualification. What rendered it worse was that his good nature—and indeed every one of his gifts, which were all of the popular order—was subservient to an assumption not only self-satisfied but obtrusive!—And yet—and yet—the objectionable character of his self-constituted judge being clear as the moon to the mind of the curate, was there not something in what he had said? This much remained undeniable at least, that when the very existence of the church was denounced as a humbug in the hearing of one who ate her bread, and was her pledged servant, his very honesty had kept that man from speaking a word in her behalf! Something must be wrong somewhere: was it in him or in the church? In him assuredly, whether in her or not. For had he not been unable to utter the simple assertion that he did believe the things which, as the mouthpiece of the church, he had been speaking in the name of the truth every Sunday—would again speak the day after to-morrow? And now the point was—WHY could he not say he believed them? He had never consciously questioned them; he did not question them now; and yet, when a forward, overbearing young infidel of a lawyer put it to him—plump—as if he were in the witness-box, or rather indeed in the dock—did he believe a word of what the church had set him to teach?—a strange something—was it honesty?—if so, how dishonest had he not hitherto been?—was it diffidence?—if so, how presumptuous his position in that church!—this nondescript something seemed to raise a "viewless obstruction" in his throat, and, having thus rendered him the first moment incapable of speaking out like a man, had taught him the next—had it?—to quibble—"like a priest" the lawyer-fellow would doubtless have said! He must go home and study Paley—or perhaps Butler's Analogy—he owed the church something, and ought to be able to strike a blow for her. Or would not Leighton be better? Or a more modern writer—say Neander, or Coleridge, or perhaps Dr. Liddon? There were thousands able to fit him out for the silencing of such foolish men as this Bascombe of the shirt-front!

Wingfold found himself filled with contempt, but the next moment was not sure whether this Bascombe or one Wingfold were the more legitimate object of it. One thing was undeniable—his friends HAD put him into the priest's office, and he had yielded to go, that he might eat a piece of bread. He had no love for it except by fits, when the beauty of an anthem, or the composition of a collect, awoke in him a faint consenting admiration, or a weak, responsive sympathy. Did he not, indeed, sometimes despise himself, and that pretty heartily, for earning his bread by work which any pious old woman could do better than he? True, he attended to his duties; not merely "did church," but his endeavour also that all things should be done decently and in order. All the same it remained a fact that if Barrister Bascombe were to stand up and assert in full congregation—as no doubt he was perfectly prepared to do—that there was no God anywhere in the universe, the Rev. Thomas Wingfold could not, on the church's part, prove to anybody that there was;—dared not, indeed, so certain would he be of discomfiture, advance a single argument on his side of the question. Was it even HIS side of the question? Could he say he believed there was a God? Or was not this all he knew—that there was a church of England, which paid him for reading public prayers to a God in whom the congregation—and himself—were supposed by some to believe, by others, Bascombe, for instance, not?

These reflections were not pleasant, especially with Sunday so near. For what if there were hundreds, yes, thousands of books, triumphantly settling every question which an over-seething and ill-instructed brain might by any chance suggest,—what could it boot?—how was a poor finite mortal, with much the ordinary faculty and capacity, and but a very small stock already stored, to set about reading, studying, understanding, mastering, appropriating the contents of those thousands of volumes necessary to the arming of him who, without pretending himself the mighty champion to seek the dragon in his den, might yet hope not to let the loathly worm swallow him, armour and all, at one gulp in the highway? Add to this that—thought of all most dismayful!—he had himself to convince first, the worst dragon of all to kill, for bare honesty's sake, in his own field; while, all the time he was arming and fighting—like the waves of the flowing tide in a sou'-wester, Sunday came in upon Sunday, roaring on his flat, defenceless shore, Sunday behind Sunday rose towering, in awful perspective, away to the verge of an infinite horizon—Sunday after Sunday of dishonesty and sham—yes, hypocrisy, far worse than any idolatry. To begin now, and in such circumstances, to study the evidences of Christianity, were about as reasonable as to send a man, whose children were crying for their dinner, off to China to make his fortune!

He laughed the idea to scorn, discovered that a gravestone in a November midnight was a cold chair for study, rose, stretched himself disconsolately, almost despairingly, looked long at the persistent solidity of the dark church and the waving line of its age-slackened ridge, which, like a mountain-range, shot up suddenly in the tower and ceased—then turning away left the houses of the dead crowded all about the house of the resurrection. At the farther gate he turned yet again, and gazed another moment on the tower. Towards the sky it towered, and led his gaze upward. There still soared, yet rested, the same quiet night with its delicate heaps of transparent blue, its cool-glowing moon, its steely stars, and its something he did not understand. He went home a little quieter of heart, as if he had heard from afar something sweet and strange.

CHAPTER VII.

THE COUSINS.

George Bascombe was a peculiar development of the present century, almost of the present generation. In the last century, beyond a doubt, the description of such a man would have been incredible. I do not mean that he was the worse or the better for that. There are types both of good and of evil which to the past would have been incredible because unintelligible.

It is very hard sometimes for a tolerably honest man, as we have just seen in the case of Wingfold, to say what he believes, and it ought to be yet harder to say what another man does not believe; therefore I shall presume no farther concerning Bascombe in this respect than to say that the thing he SEEMED most to believe was that he had a mission to destroy the beliefs of everybody else. Whence he derived this mission he would not have thought a reasonable question—would have answered that, if any man knew any truth unknown to another, understood any truth better, or could present it more clearly than another, the truth itself was his commission of apostleship. And his stand was indubitably a firm one. Only there was the question—whether his presumed commission was verily truth or no. It must be allowed that a good deal turns upon that.

According to the judgment of some men who thought they knew him, Bascombe was as yet—I will not say incapable of distinguishing, but careless of the distinction between—not a fact and a law, perhaps, but a law and a truth. They said also that he inveighed against the beliefs of other people, without having ever seen more than a distorted shadow of those beliefs—some of them he was not capable of seeing, they said—only capable of denying. Now while he would have been perfectly justified, they said, in asserting that he saw no truth in the things he denied, was he justifiable in concluding that his not seeing a thing was a proof of its non-existence—anything more, in fact, than a presumption against its existence? or in denouncing every man who said he believed this or that which Bascombe did not believe, as either a knave or a fool, if not both in one? He would, they said, judge anybody—a Shakespeare, a Bacon, a Milton—without a moment's hesitation or a quiver of reverence—judge men who, beside him, were as the living ocean to a rose-diamond. If he was armed in honesty, the rivets were of self-satisfaction. The suit, they allowed, was adamantine, unpierceable.

That region of a man's nature which has to do with the unknown was in Bascombe shut off by a wall without chink or cranny; he was unaware of its existence. He had come out of the darkness, and was going back into the darkness; all that lay between, plain and clear, he had to do with—nothing more. He could not present to himself the idea of a man who found it impossible to live without some dealings with the supernal. To him a man's imagination was of no higher calling than to amuse him with its vagaries. He did not know, apparently, that Imagination had been the guide to all the physical discoveries which he worshipped, therefore could not reason that perhaps she might be able to carry a glimmering light even into the forest of the supersensible.

How far he was original in the views he propounded, will, to those who understand the times of which I write, be plain enough. The lively reception of another man's doctrine, especially if it comes over water or across a few ages of semi-oblivion, and has to be gathered with occasional help from a dictionary, raises many a man, in his own esteem, to the same rank with its first propounder; after which he will propound it so heartily himself as to forget the difference, and love it as his own child.

It may seem strange that the son of a clergyman should take such a part in the world's affairs, but one who observes will discover that, at college at least, the behaviour of sons of clergymen resembles in general as little as that of any, and less than that of most, the behaviour enjoined by the doctrines their fathers have to teach. The cause of this is matter of consideration for those fathers. In Bascombe's case, it must be mentioned also that, instead of taking freedom from prejudice as a portion of the natural accomplishment of a gentleman, he prided himself upon it, and THEREFORE would often go dead against the things presumed to be held by THE CLOTH, long before he had begun to take his position as an iconoclast.

Lest I should, however, tire my reader with the delineations of a character not of the most interesting, I shall, for the present, only add that Bascombe had persuaded himself, and without much difficulty, that he was one of the prophets of a new order of things. At Cambridge he had been so regarded by a few who had lauded him as a mighty foe to humbug—and in some true measure he deserved the praise. Since then he had found a larger circle, and had even radiated of his light, such, as it was, from the centres of London editorial offices. But all I have to do with now is the fact that he had grown desirous to add his cousin, Helen Lingard, to the number of those who believed in him, and over whom, therefore, he exercised a prophet's influence.

No doubt it added much to the attractiveness of the intellectual game that the hunt was on the home grounds of such a proprietress as Helen—a handsome, a gifted, and, above all, a ladylike young woman. To do Bascombe justice, the fact that she was an heiress also had very little weight in the matter. If he had ever had any thought of marrying her, that thought was not consciously present to him when first he became aware of his wish to convert her to his views of life. But, although he was not in love with her, he admired her, and believed he saw in her one that resembled himself.

As to Helen, although she was no more conscious of cause of self-dissatisfaction than her cousin, she was not therefore positively self-satisfied like him. For that her mind was not active enough.

If it seem, as it may, to some of my readers, difficult to believe that she should have come to her years without encountering any questions, giving life to any aspirations, or even forming any opinions that could rightly be called her own, I would remind them that she had always had good health, and that her intellectual faculties had been kept in full and healthy exercise, nor had once afforded the suspicion of a tendency towards artistic utterance in any direction. She was no mere dabbler in anything: in music, for instance, she had studied thorough bass, and studied it well; yet her playing was such as I have already described it. She understood perspective, and could copy an etching, in pen and ink, to a hair's-breadth, yet her drawing was hard and mechanical. She was pretty much at home in Euclid, and thoroughly enjoyed a geometric relation, but had never yet shown her English master the slightest pleasure in an analogy, or the smallest sympathy with any poetry higher than such as very properly delights schoolboys. Ten thousand things she knew without wondering at one of them. Any attempt to rouse her admiration, she invariably received with quiet intelligence but no response. Yet her drawing-master was convinced there lay a large soul asleep somewhere below the calm grey morning of that wide-awake yet reposeful intelligence.

As far as she knew—only she had never thought anything about it—she was in harmony with creation animate and inanimate, and for what might or might not be above creation, or at the back, or the heart, or the mere root of it, how could she think about a something the idea of which had never yet been presented to her by love or philosophy, or even curiosity? As for any influence from the public offices of religion, a contented soul may glide through them all for a long life, unstruck to the last, buoyant and evasive as a bee amongst hailstones. And now her cousin, unsolicited, was about to assume, if she should permit him, the unspiritual direction of her being, so that she need never be troubled from the quarter of the unknown.

Mrs. Ramshorn's house had formerly been the manor-house, and, although it now stood in an old street, with only a few yards of ground between it and the road, it had a large and ancient garden behind it. A large garden of any sort is valuable, but an ancient garden is invaluable, and this one had retained a very antique loveliness. The quaint memorials of its history lived on into the new, changed, unsympathetic time, and stood there, aged, modest, and unabashed. Yet not one of the family had ever cared for it on the ground of its old-fashionedness; its preservation was owing merely to the fact that their gardener was blessed with a wholesome stupidity rendering him incapable of unlearning what his father, who had been gardener there before him, had had marvellous difficulty in teaching him. We do not half appreciate the benefits to the race that spring from honest dulness. The CLEVER people are the ruin of everything.

Into this garden, Bascombe walked the next morning, after breakfast, and Helen, who, next to the smell of a fir-wood fire, honestly liked the odour of a good cigar, spying him from her balcony, which was the roof of the veranda, where she was trimming the few remaining chrysanthemums that stood outside the window of her room, ran down the little wooden stair that led from it to the garden, and joined him. Nothing could just at present have been more to his mind.

CHAPTER VIII.

THE GARDEN.

"Take a cigar, Helen?" said George.

"No, thank you," answered Helen; "I like it diluted."

"I don't see why ladies should not have things strong as men."

"Not if they don't want them. You can't enjoy everything—I mean, one can't have the strong and the delicate both at once. I don't believe a smoker can have the same pleasure in smelling a rose that I have."

"Isn't it a pity we never can compare sensations?"

"I don't think it matters much: everyone would have to keep to his own after all."

"That's good, Helen! If ever man try to humbug you, he will find he has lost his stirrups. If only there were enough like you left in this miserable old hulk of a creation!"

It was an odd thing that when in the humour of finding fault, Bascombe would not unfrequently speak of the cosmos as a creation. He was himself unaware of the curious fact.

"You seem to have a standing quarrel with the creation, George! Yet one might think you had as little ground as most people to complain of your portion in it," said Helen.

"Well, you know, I don't complain for myself. I don't pretend to think I am specially ill-used. But I am not everybody. And then there's such a lot of born-fools in it!"

"If they are born-fools they can't help it."

"That may be; only it makes it none the pleasanter for other people; but, unfortunately, they are not the only or the worst sort of fools. For one born-fool there are a thousand wilful ones. For one man that will honestly face an honest argument, there are ten thousand that will dishonestly shirk it. There's that curate-fellow now—Wingfold I think aunt called him—look at him now!"

"I can't see much in him to rouse indignation," said Helen. "He seems a very inoffensive man."

"I don't call it inoffensive when a man sells himself to the keeping up of a system that——"

Here Bascombe checked himself, remembering that a sudden attack upon what was, at least, the more was the pity, a time-honoured system, might rouse a woman's prejudices; and as Helen had already listened to a large amount of undermining remark without perceiving the direction of his tunnels, he resolved, before venturing an open assault, to make sure that those prejudices stood, lightly borne, over an abyss of seething objection. He had had his experiences as the prophet-pioneer of glad tidings to the nations, and had before now, although such weakness he could not anticipate in Helen, seen one whom he considered a most promising pupil, turned suddenly away in a storm of terror and disgust.

"What a folly is it now," he instantly resumed, leaving the general and attacking a particular, "to think to make people good by promises and threats—promises of a heaven that would bore the dullest among them to death, and threats of a hell the very idea of which, if only half conceived, would be enough to paralyse every nerve of healthy action in the human system!"

"All nations have believed in a future state, either of reward or punishment," objected Helen.

"Mere Brocken-spectres of their own approbation or disapprobation of themselves. And whither has it brought the race?"

"What then would you substitute for it, George?"

"Why substitute anything? Ought not men be good to one another because they are made up of ones and others? Do you or I need threats and promises to make us kind? And what right have we to judge others worse than ourselves? Mutual compassion," he went on, blowing out a mouthful of smoke and then swelling his big chest with a huge lungful of air, "might be sufficient to teach poor ephemerals kindness and consideration enough to last their time."

"But how would you bring such reflections to bear?" asked Helen, pertinently.

"I would reason thus: You must consider that you are but a part of the whole, and that whatever you do to hurt the whole, or injure any of its parts, will return upon you who form one of those parts."

"How would that influence the man whose favourite amusement is to beat his wife!"

"Not at all, I grant you. But that man is what he is from being born and bred under a false and brutal system. Having deluged his delicate brain with the poisonous fumes of adulterated liquor, and so roused all the terrors of a phantom-haunted imagination, he sees hostile powers above watching for his fall, and fiery ruin beneath gaping to receive him, and in pure despair acts like the madman the priests and the publicans have made him. Helen," continued Bascombe with solemnity, regarding her fixedly, "to deliver the race from the horrors of such falsehoods, which by no means operate only on the vulgar and brutal, for to how many of the most refined and delicate of human beings are not their lives rendered bitter by the evil suggestions of lying systems—I care not what they are called—philosophy, religion, society, I care not?—to deliver men, I say, from such ghouls of the human brain, were indeed to have lived! and in the consciousness of having spent his life in the slaying of such dragons, a man may well go from the nameless past into the nameless future rejoicing, careless even if his poor length of days be shortened by his labours to leave blessing behind him, and, full of courage even in the moment of final dissolution, cast her mockery back into the face of mocking Life, and die her enemy, and the friend of Death!"

George's language was a little confused. Perhaps he mingled his ideas a little for Helen's sake—or rather for obscurity's sake. Anyhow, the mournful touch in it was not his own, but taken from the poems of certain persons whose opinions resembled his, but floated on the surface of mighty and sad hearts. Tall, stately, comfortable Helen walked composedly by his side, softly shared his cigar, and thought what a splendid pleader he would make. Perhaps to her it sounded rather finer than it was, for its tone of unselfishness, the aroma of self-devotion that floated about it, pleased and attracted her. Was not here a youth in the prime of being and the dawn of success, handsome, and smoking the oldest of Havannahs, who, so far from being enamoured of his own existence, was anxious and careful about that of less favoured mortals, for whose welfare indeed he was willing to sacrifice his life?—nothing less could be what he meant. And how fine he looked as he said it, with his head erect, and his nostrils quivering like those of a horse! For his honesty, that was self-evident!

Perhaps, had she been capable of looking into it, the self-evident honesty might have resolved itself into this—that he thoroughly believed in himself; that he meant what he said; and that he offered her nothing he did not prize and cleave to as his own.

To one who had read Darwin, and had chanced to see them as they walked in their steady, stately young life among the ancient cedars and clipped yews of the garden, with the rags and tatters of the ruined summer hanging over and around them, they must have looked as fine an instance of natural selection as the world had to show. And now in truth for the first time, with any shadow of purpose, that is, did the thought of Helen as a wife occur to Bascombe. She listened so well, was so ready to take what he presented to her, was evidently so willing to become a pupil, that he began to say to himself that here was the very woman made—no, not made, that implied a maker—

but for him, without the MADE; that is, if ever he should bring himself by marriage to limit the freedom to which man, the crown of the world, the blossom of nature, the cauliflower of the spine, was predestined or doomed, without will in himself or beyond himself, from an eternity of unthinking matter, ever producing what was better than itself in the prolific darkness of non-intent.

CHAPTER IX.

THE PARK.

At the bottom of Mrs. Ramshorn's garden was a deep sunk fence, which allowed a large meadow, a fragment of what had once been the manor-park, to belong, so far as the eye was concerned, to the garden. Nor was this all, for in the sunk fence was a door with a little tunnel, by which they could pass at once from the garden to the meadow. So, the day being wonderfully fine, Bascombe proposed to his cousin a walk in the park, the close-paling of which, with a small door in it, whereto Mrs. Ramshorn had the privilege of a key, was visible on the other side of the meadow. The two keys had but to be fetched from the house, and in a few minutes they were in the park. The turf was dry, the air was still, and although the woods were very silent, and looked mournfully bare, the grass drew nearer to the roots of the trees, and the sunshine filled them with streaks of gold, blending lovelily with the bright green of the moss that patched the older stems. Neither horses nor dogs say to themselves, I suppose, that the sunshine makes them glad, yet both are happier, after the rules of equine and canine existence, on a bright day: neither Helen nor George could have understood a poem of Keats—not to say Wordsworth—(I do not mean they would not have fancied they did)— and yet the soul of nature that dwelt in these common shows did not altogether fail of influence upon them.

"I wonder what the birds do with themselves all the winter," said Helen.

"Eat berries, and make the best of it," answered George.

"I mean what becomes of them all. We see so few of them."

"About as many as you see in summer. Because you hear them you fancy you see them."

"But there is so little to hide them in winter."

"Little is wanted to hide our dusky creatures."

"They must have a hard time of it in frost and snow."

"Oh! I don't know," returned George. "They enjoy life on the whole, I believe. It ain't such a very bad sort of a world as some people would have it. Nature is cruel enough in some of her arrangements, it can't be denied. She don't scruple to carry out her plans. It is nothing to her that for the life of one great monster of a high-priest, millions upon millions of submissive little fishes should be sacrificed; and then if anybody come within the teeth of her machinery, don't she mangle him finely—with her fevers and her agues and her convulsions and consumptions and what not? But still, barring her own necessities, and the consequences of man's ignorance and foolhardiness, she is on the whole rather a good-natured old woman, and scatters a deal of tolerably fair enjoyment around her."

"One WOULD think the birds must be happy in summer, at least, to hear them sing," corroborated Helen.

"Yes, or to see them stripping a hawthorn bush in winter—always provided the cat or the hawk don't get hold of them. With that nature does not trouble herself. Well, it's soon over—with all of us, and that's a comfort. If men would only get rid of their cats and hawks,—such as the fancy for instance, that all their suffering comes of the will of a malignant power! That is the kind of thing that makes the misery of the world!"

"I don't quite see———" began Helen.

"We were talking about the birds in winter," interrupted George, careful not to swell too suddenly any of the air-bags with which he would float Helen's belief. He knew wisely, and he knew how, to leave a hint to work while it was yet not half understood. By the time it was understood, it would have grown a little familiar: the supposed pup when it turned out a cub, would not be so terrible as if it had presented itself at once as leonate.

And so they wandered across the park, talking easily.

"They've got on a good way since I was here last," said George, as they came in sight of the new house the new earl was building. "But they don't seem much in a hurry with it either."

"Aunt says it is twenty years since the foundations were laid by the uncle of the present earl," said Helen; "and then for some reason or other the thing was dropped."

"Was there no house on the place before?"

"Oh! yes—not much of a house, though."

"And they pulled it down, I suppose."

"No; it stands there still."

"Where?"

"Down in the hollow there—over those trees—about the worst place they could have built in. Surely you have seen it! Poldie and I used to run all over it."

"No, I never saw it. Was it empty then?"

"Yes, or almost. I can remember some little attention paid to the garden, but none to the house. It is just falling slowly to pieces. Would you like to see it?"

"That I should," returned Bascombe, who was always ready for any new impression on his sensorium, and away they went to look at the old house of Glaston as it was called, after some greatly older and probably fortified place.

In the hollow all the water of the park gathered to a lake before finding its way to the river Lythe. This lake was at the bottom of the old garden, and the house at the top of it. The garden was walled on the two sides, and the walls ran right down to the lake. There were wonderful legends current amongst the children of Glaston concerning that lake, its depth, and the creatures in it; and one terrible story, which had been made a ballad of, about a lady drowned in a sack, whose ghost might still be seen when the moon was old, haunting the gardens and the house. Hence it came that none of them went near it, except those few whose appetites for adventure now and then grew keen enough to prevent their imaginations from rousing more fear than supplied the proper relish of danger. The house itself even those few never dared to enter.

Not so had it been with Helen and Leopold. The latter had imagination enough to receive everything offered, but Helen was the leader, and she had next to none. In her childhood she had heard the tales alluded to from her nurses, but she had been to school since, and had learned not to believe them; and certainly she was not one to be frightened at what she did not believe. So when Leopold came in the holidays, the place was one of their favoured haunts, and they knew every cubic yard in the house.

"Here," said Helen to her cousin, as she opened the door in a little closet, and showed a dusky room which had no window but a small one high up in the wall of a back staircase, "here is one room into which I never could get Poldie without the greatest trouble. I gave it up at last, he always trembled so till he got out again. I will show you such a curious place at the other end of it."

She led the way to a closet similar to that by which they had entered, and directed Bascombe how to raise a trap which filled all the floor of it so that it did not show. Under the trap was a sort of well, big enough to hold three upon emergency.

"If only they could contrive to breathe," said George. "It looks ugly. If it had but a brain and a tongue it could tell tales."

"Come," said Helen. "I don't know how it is, but I don't like the look of it myself now. Let us get into the open air again."

Ascending from the hollow, and passing through a deep belt of trees that surrounded it, they came again to the open park, and by-and-by reached the road that led from the lodge to the new building, upon which they presently encountered a strange couple.

CHAPTER X.

THE DWARFS.

The moment they had passed them, George turned to his cousin with a countenance which bore moral indignation mingled with disgust. The healthy instincts of the elect of his race were offended by the sight of such physical failures, such mockeries of humanity as those.

The woman was little if anything over four feet in height. She was crooked, had a high shoulder, and walked like a crab, one leg being shorter than the other. Her companion walked quite straight, with a certain appearance of dignity which he neither assumed nor could have avoided, and which gave his gait the air of a march. He was not an inch taller than the woman, had broad, square shoulders, pigeon-breast, and invisible neck. He was twice her age, and they seemed father and daughter. They heard his breathing, loud with asthma, as they went by.

"Poor things!" said Helen, with cold kindness.

"It is shameful!" said George, in a tone of righteous anger. "Such creatures have no right to existence. The horrid manakin!"

"But, George!" said Helen, in expostulation, "the poor wretch can't help his deformity."

"No; but what right had he to marry and perpetuate such odious misery!"

"You are too hasty: the young woman is his niece."

"She ought to have been strangled the moment she was born—for the sake of humanity. Monsters ought not to live."

"Unfortunately they have all got mothers," said Helen; and something in her face made him fear he had gone too far.

"Don't mistake me, dear Helen," he said. "I would neither starve nor drown them after they had reached the faculty of resenting such treatment—of the justice of which," he added, smiling, "I am afraid it would be hard to convince them. But such people actually marry —I have known cases,—and that ought to be provided against by suitable enactments and penalties."

"And so," rejoined Helen, "because they are unhappy already, you would heap unhappiness upon them?"

"Now, Helen, you must not be unfair to me any more than to your hunchbacks. It is the good of the many I seek, and surely that is better than the good of the few."

"What I object to is, that it should be at the expense of the few—who are least able to bear it."

"The expense is trifling," said Bascombe. "Grant that it would be better for society that no such—or rather put it this way: grant that it would be well for each individual that goes to make up society that he were neither deformed, sickly, nor idiotic, and you mean the same that I do. A given space of territory under given conditions will always maintain a certain number of human beings; therefore such a law as I propose would not mean that the number drawing the breath of heaven should, to take the instance before us in illustration, be two less, but that a certain two of them should not be such as he or she who passed now, creatures whose existence is a burden to them, but such as you and I, Helen, who may say without presumption that we are no disgrace to Nature's handicraft."

Helen was not sensitive. She neither blushed nor cast down her eyes. But his tenets, thus expounded, had nothing very repulsive in them so far as she saw, and she made no further objection to them.

As they walked up the garden again, through the many lingering signs of a more stately if less luxurious existence than that of their generation, she was calmly listening to a lecture on the ground of law, namely, the resignation of certain personal rights for the securing of other and more important ones: she understood, was mildly interested, and entirely satisfied.

They seated themselves in the summer-house, a little wooden room under the down-sloping boughs of a huge cedar, and pursued their conversation— or rather Bascombe pursued his monologue. A lively girl would in all probability have been bored to death by him, but Helen was not a lively girl, and was not bored at all. Ere they went into the house she had heard, amongst a hundred other things of wisdom, his views concerning crime and punishment—with which, good and bad, true and false, I shall not trouble my reader, except in regard to one point—that of the obligation to punish. Upon this point he was severe.

No person, he said, ought to allow any weakness of pity to prevent him from bringing to punishment the person who broke the laws upon which the well-being of the community depended. A man must remember that the good of the whole, and not the fate of the individual, was to be regarded.

It was altogether a notable sort of tête-à-tête between two such perfect specimens of the race, and as at length they entered the house, they professed to each other to have much enjoyed their walk.

Holding the opinions he did, Bascombe was in one thing inconsistent: he went to "divine service" on the Sunday with his aunt and cousin—not to humour Helen's prejudices, but those of Mrs. Ramshorn, who, belonging, as

I have said, to the profession, had strong opinions as to the wickedness of not going to church. It was of no use, he said to himself, trying to upset her ideas, for to succeed would only be to make her miserable, and his design was to make the race happy. In the grand old Abbey, therefore, they heard together morning prayers, the Litany, and the Communion, all in one, after a weariful and lazy modern custom not yet extinct, and then a dull, sensible sermon, short, and tolerably well read, on the duty of forgiveness of injuries.

I dare say it did most of the people present a little good, undefinable as the faint influences of starlight, to sit under that "high embowed roof," within that vast artistic isolation, through whose mighty limiting the boundless is embodied, and we learn to feel the awful infinitude of the parent space out of which it is scooped. I dare also say that the tones of the mellow old organ spoke to something in many of the listeners that lay deeper far than the plummet of their self-knowledge had ever sounded. I think also that the prayers, the reading of which, in respect of intelligence, was admirable, were not only regarded as sacred utterances, but felt to be soothing influences by not a few of those who made not the slightest effort to follow them with their hearts; and I trust that on the whole their church-going tended rather to make them better than to harden them. But as to the main point, the stirring up of the children of the Highest to lay hold of the skirts of their Father's robe, the waking of the individual conscience to say I WILL ARISE, and the strengthening of the captive Will to break its bonds and stand free in the name of the eternal creating Freedom—for nothing of that was there any special provision. This belonged, in the nature of things, to the sermon, in which, if anywhere, the voice of the indwelling Spirit might surely be heard—out of his holy temple, if indeed that be the living soul of man, as St. Paul believed; but there was no sign that the preacher regarded his office as having any such end, although in his sermon lingered the rudimentary tokens that such must have been the original intent of pulpit-utterance.

On the way home, Bascombe made some objections to the discourse, partly to show his aunt that he had been attending. He admitted that one might forgive and forget what did not come within the scope of the law, but, as he had said to Helen before, a man was bound, he said, to punish the wrong which through him affected the community.

"George," said his aunt, "I differ from you there. Nobody ought to go to the law to punish an injury. I would forgive ever so many before I would run the risk of the law. But as to FORGETTING an injury—some injuries at least—no, that I never would!—And I don't believe, let the young man say what he will, that that is required of anyone."

Helen said nothing. She had no enemies to forgive, no wrongs worth remembering, and was not interested in the question. She thought it a very good sermon indeed.

When Bascombe left for London in the morning, he carried with him the lingering rustle of silk, the odour of lavender, and a certain blueness, not of the sky, which seemed to have something behind it, as never did the sky to him. He had never met woman so worthy of being his mate, either as regarded the perfection of her form, or the hidden development of her brain—evident in her capacity for the reception of truth, as his own cousin, Helen Lingard. Might not the relationship account for the fact?

Helen thought nothing to correspond. She considered George a fine manly fellow. What bold and original ideas he had about everything! Her brother was a baby to him! But then Leopold was such a love of a boy! Such eyes and such a smile were not to be seen on this side the world. Helen liked her cousin, was attached to her aunt, but loved her brother Leopold, and loved nobody else. His Hindoo mother, high of caste, had given him her lustrous eyes and pearly smile, which, the first moment she saw him, won his sister's heart. He was then but eight years old, and she but eleven. Since then, he had been brought up by his father's elder brother, who had the family estate in Yorkshire, but he had spent part of all his holidays with her, and they often wrote to each other. Of late indeed his letters had not been many, and a rumour had reached her that he was not doing quite satisfactorily at Cambridge, but she explained it away to the full contentment of her own heart, and went on building such castles as her poor aerolithic skill could command, with Leopold ever and always as the sharer of her self-expansion.

CHAPTER XI.

THE CURATE AT HOME.

If we could arrive at the feelings of a fish of the northern ocean around which the waters suddenly rose to tropical temperature, and swarmed with strange forms of life, uncouth and threatening, we should have a fair symbol of the mental condition in which Thomas Wingfold now found himself. The spiritual fluid in which his being floated had become all at once more potent, and he was in consequence uncomfortable. A certain intermittent stinging, as if from the flashes of some moral electricity, had begun to pass in various directions through the crude and chaotic mass he called himself, and he felt strangely restless. It never occurred to him—as how should it?—that he might have commenced undergoing the most marvellous of all changes,— one so marvellous, indeed, that for a man to foreknow its result or understand what he was passing through, would be more strange than that a caterpillar should recognise in the rainbow-winged butterfly hovering over the flower at whose leaf he was gnawing, the perfected idea of his own potential self—I mean the change of being born again. Nor were the symptoms such as would necessarily have suggested, even to a man experienced in the natural history of the infinite, that the process had commenced.

A restless night followed his reflections in the churchyard, and he did not wake at all comfortable. Not that ever he had been in the way of feeling comfortable. To him life had not been a land flowing with milk and honey. He had had few smiles, and not many of those grasps of the hand which let a man know another man is near him in the battle—for had it not been something of a battle, how could he have come to the age of six-and-twenty without being worse than he was? He would not have said: "All these have I kept from my youth up;" but I can say that for several of them he had shown fight, although only One knew anything of it. This morning, then, it was not merely that he did not feel comfortable: he was consciously uncomfortable. Things were getting too hot for him. That infidel fellow had poked several most awkward questions at him—yes, into him, and a good many more had in him—self arisen to meet them. Usually he lay a little while before he came to himself; but this morning he came to himself at once, and not liking the interview, jumped out of bed as if he had hoped to leave himself there behind him.

He had always scorned lying, until one day, when still a boy at school, he suddenly found that he had told a lie, after which he hated it—yet now, if he was to believe—ah! whom? did not the positive fellow and his own conscience say the same thing?—his profession, his very life was a lie! the very bread he ate grew on the rank fields of falsehood!—No, no; it was absurd! it could not be! What had he done to find himself damned to such a depth? Yet the thing must be looked to. He batht himself without remorse and never even shivered, though the water in his tub was bitterly cold, dressed with more haste than precision, hurried over his breakfast, neglected his newspaper, and took down a volume of early church history. But he could not read: the thing was hopeless—utterly. With the wolves of doubt and the jackals of shame howling at his heels, how could he start for a thousand-mile race! For God's sake give him a weapon to turn and face them with! Evidence! all of it that was to be had, was but such as one man received, another man refused; and the popular acceptance was worth no more in respect of Christianity than of Mahometanism, for how many had given the subject at all better consideration than himself? And there was Sunday with its wolves and jackals, and but a hedge between! He did not so much mind reading the prayers: he was not accountable for what was in them, although it was bad enough to stand up and read them. Happy thing he was not a dissenter, for then he would have had to pretend to pray from his own soul, which would have been too horrible! But there was the sermon! That at least was supposed to contain, or to be presented as containing, his own sentiments. Now what were his sentiments? For the life of him he could not tell. Had he ANY sentiments, any opinions, any beliefs, any unbeliefs? He had plenty of sermons—old, yellow, respectable sermons, not lithographed, neither composed by mind nor copied out by hand unknown, but in the neat writing of his old D.D. uncle, so legible that he never felt it necessary to read them over beforehand—just saw that he had the right one. A hundred and fifty-seven such sermons, the odd one for the year that began on a Sunday, of unquestionable orthodoxy, had his kind old uncle left him in his will, with the feeling probably that he was not only setting him up in sermons for life, but giving him a fair start as well in the race of which a stall in some high cathedral was the goal. For his own part he had never made a sermon, at least never one he had judged worth preaching to a congregation. He had rather a high idea, he thought, of preaching, and these sermons of his uncle he considered really excellent. Some of them, however, were altogether doctrinal, some very polemical: of such he must now beware. He would see of what kind was the next in order; he would read it and make sure it contained nothing he was not, in some degree at least, prepared to hold his face to and defend—if he could not absolutely swear he believed it purely true.

He did as resolved. The first he took up was in defence of the Athanasian creed! That would not do. He tried another. That was upon the Inspiration of the Scriptures. He glanced through it—found Moses on a level with St. Paul, and Jonah with St. John, and doubted greatly. There might be a sense—but—! No, he would not meddle with it. He tried a third: that was on the

Authority of the Church. It would not do. He had read each of all these sermons, at least once, to a congregation, with perfect composure and following indifference, if not peace of mind, but now he could not come on one with which he was even in sympathy—not to say one of which he was certain that it was more true than false. At last he took up the odd one—that which could come into use but once in a week of years—and this was the sermon Bascombe heard and commented upon. Having read it over, and found nothing to compromise him with his conscience, which was like an irritable man trying to find his way in a windy wood by means of a broken lantern, he laid all the rest aside and felt a little relieved.

Wingfold had never neglected the private duty of a clergyman in regard of morning and evening devotions, but was in the habit of dressing and undressing his soul with the help of certain chosen contents of the prayer-book—a somewhat circuitous mode of communicating with Him who was so near him,—that is, if St. Paul was right in saying that he lived, and moved, and was, IN Him; but that Saturday he knelt by his bedside at noon, and began to pray or try to pray as he had never prayed or tried to pray before. The perplexed man cried out within the clergyman, and pressed for some acknowledgment from God of the being he had made.

But—was it strange to tell? or if strange, was it not the most natural result nevertheless?—almost the same moment he began to pray in this truer fashion, the doubt rushed up in him like a torrent-spring from the fountains of the great deep—Was there—could there be a God at all? a real being who might actually hear his prayer? In this crowd of houses and shops and churches, amidst buying and selling, and ploughing and praising and backbiting, this endless pursuit of ends and of means to ends, while yet even the wind that blew where it listed blew under laws most fixed, and the courses of the stars were known to a hair's-breadth, —was there—could there be a silent invisible God working his own will in it all? Was there a driver to that chariot whose multitudinous horses seemed tearing away from the pole in all directions? and was he indeed, although invisible and inaudible, guiding that chariot, sure as the flight of a comet, straight to its goal? Or was there a soul to that machine whose myriad wheels went grinding on and on, grinding the stars into dust, matter into man, and man into nothingness? Was there—could there be a living heart to the universe that did positively hear him—poor, misplaced, dishonest, ignorant Thomas Wingfold, who had presumed to undertake a work he neither could perform nor had the courage to forsake, when out of the misery of the grimy little cellar of his consciousness he cried aloud for light and something to make a man of him? For now that Thomas had begun to doubt like an honest being, every ugly thing within him began to show itself to his awakened probity.

But honest and of good parentage as the doubts were, no sooner had they shown themselves than the wings of the ascending prayers fluttered feebly and failed. They sank slowly, fell, and lay as dead, while all the wretchedness of his position rushed back upon him with redoubled inroad. Here was a man who could not pray, and yet must go and read prayers and preach in the old attesting church, as if he too were of those who knew something of the secrets of the Almighty, and could bring out from his treasury, if not things new and surprising, then things old and precious! Ought he not to send round the bell-man to cry aloud that there would be no service? But what right had he to lay his troubles, the burden of his dishonesty, upon the shoulders of them who faithfully believed, and who looked to him to break to them their daily bread? And would not any attempt at a statement of the reasons he had for such an outrageous breach of all decorum be taken for a denial of those things concerning which he only desired most earnestly to know that they were true. For he had received from somewhere, he knew not how or whence, a genuine prejudice in favour of Christianity, while of those refractions and distorted reflexes of it which go by its name and rightly disgust many, he had had few of the tenets thrust upon his acceptance.

Thus into the dark pool of his dull submissive life, the bold words of the unbeliever had fallen—a dead stone perhaps, but causing a thousand motions in the living water. Question crowded upon question, and doubt upon doubt, until he could bear it no longer, and starting from the floor on which at last he had sunk prostrate, he rushed in all but involuntary haste from the house, and scarcely knew where he was until, in a sort, he came to himself some little distance from the town, wandering hurriedly in field-paths.

CHAPTER XII.

AN INCIDENT.

It was a fair morning of All Hallows' summer. The trees were nearly despoiled, but the grass was green, and there was a memory of spring in the low sad sunshine: even the sunshine, the gladdest thing in creation, is sad sometimes. There was no wind, nothing to fight with, nothing to turn his mind from its own miserable perplexities. How endlessly his position as a clergyman, he thought, added to his miseries! Had he been a man unpledged, he could have taken his own time to think out the truths of his relations; as it was, he felt like a man in a coffin: out he must get, but had not room to make a single vigorous effort for freedom! It did not occur to him yet that, uupressed from without, his honesty unstung, he might have taken more time to find out where he was than would have been either honest or healthful.

He came to a stile where his path joined another that ran both ways, and there seated himself, just as the same strange couple I have already described as met by Miss Lingard and Mr. Bascombe approached and went by. After they had gone a good way, he caught sight of something lying in the path, and going to pick it up, found it was a small manuscript volume.

With the pleasurable instinct of service, he hastened after them. They heard him, and turning waited his approach. He took off his hat, and presenting the book to the young woman, asked if she had dropped it. Possibly, had they been ordinary people of the class to which they seemed to belong, he would not have uncovered to them, for he naturally shrunk from what might be looked upon as a display of courtesy, but their deformity rendered it imperative. Her face flushed so at sight of the book, that, in order to spare her uneasiness, Wingfold could not help saying with a smile,

"Do not be alarmed: I have not read one word of it."

She returned his smile with much sweetness, and said—

"I see I need not have been afraid."

Her companion joined in thanks and apologies for having caused him so much trouble. Wingfold assured them it had been but a pleasure. It was far from a scrutinizing look with which he regarded them, but the interview left him with the feeling that their faces were refined and intelligent, and their speech was good. Again he lifted his rather shabby hat, the man responded with equal politeness in removing from a great grey head one rather better, and they turned from each other and went their ways, the sight of their malformation arousing in the curate no such questions as those with which it had agitated the tongue, if not the heart, of George Bascombe, to widen the scope of his perplexities. He had heard the loud breathing of the man, and seen the projecting eyes of the woman, but he never said to himself therefore that they were more hardly dealt with than he. Had such a thought occurred to him, he would have comforted the pain of his sympathy with the reflection that at least neither of them was a curate of the church of England who knew positively nothing of the foundation upon which that church professed to stand.

How he got through the Sunday he never could have told. What times a man may get through—he knows not how! As soon as it was over, it was all a mist—from which gleamed or gloomed large the face of George Bascombe with its keen unbelieving eyes and scornful lips. All the time he was reading the prayers and lessons, all the time he was reading his uncle's sermon, he had not only been aware of those eyes, but aware also of what lay behind them—seeing and reading the reflex of himself in Bascombe's brain; but nothing more whatever could he recall.

Like finger-posts dim seen, on a moorland journey, through the gathering fogs, Sunday after Sunday passed. I will not request my reader to accompany me across the confusions upon which was blowing that wind whose breath was causing a world to pass from chaos to cosmos. One who has ever gone through any experience of the kind himself, will be able to imagine it; to one who has not, my descriptions would be of small service: he would but shrink from the representation as diseased and of no general interest. And he would be so far right, that the interest in such things must be most particular and individual, or none at all.

The weeks passed and seemed to bring him no light, only increased earnestness in the search after it. Some assurance he must find soon, else he would resign his curacy, and look out for a situation as tutor.

Of course all this he ought to have gone through long ago! But how can a man go through anything till his hour be come? Saul of Tarsus was sitting at the feet of Gamaliel when our Lord said to his apostles—"Yea, the time cometh, that whosoever killeth you will think that he doeth God service." Wingfold had all this time been skirting the wall of the kingdom of heaven without even knowing that there was a wall there, not to say seeing a gate in it. The fault lay with those who had brought him up to the church as to the profession of medicine, or the bar, or the drapery business—as if it lay on one level of choice with other human callings. Nor were the honoured of the church who had taught him free from blame, who never warned him to put his shoes from off his feet for the holiness of the ground. But how were they to warn him, if they had sowed and reaped and gathered into barns on that ground, and had never discovered therein treasure more holy than libraries, incomes, and the visits of royalty? As to visions of truth that make a man sigh with joy, and enlarge his heart with more than human tenderness—how many of those men had ever found such treasure in the fields of the church? How many of them knew save by hearsay whether there be any Holy Ghost! How then were they to warn other men from the dangers of following in their footsteps and becoming such as they? Where, in a general ignorance and community of fault, shall we begin to blame? Wingfold had no time to accuse anyone after the first gush of bitterness. He had to awake from the dead and cry for light, and was soon in the bitter agony of the cataleptic struggle between life and death.

He thought afterwards, when the time had passed, that surely in this period of darkness he had been visited and upheld by a power whose presence and even influence escaped his consciousness. He knew not how else he could have got through it. Also he remembered that strange helps had come to him; that the aspects of nature then wonderfully softened towards him, that then first he began to feel sympathy with her ways and shows, and to see in them all the working of a diffused humanity. He remembered how once a hawthorn bud set him weeping; and how once, as he went miserable to church, a child looked up in his face and smiled, and how in the strength of that smile he had walked boldly to the lectern.

He never knew how long he had been in the strange birth agony, in which the soul is as it were at once the mother that bears and the child that is born.

CHAPTER XIII.

A REPORT OF PROGRESS.

In the meantime George Bascombe came and went; every visit he showed clearer notions as to what he was for, and what he was against; every visit he found Helen more worthy and desirable than theretofore, and flattered himself he made progress in the conveyance of his opinions and judgments over into her mind. His various accomplishments went far in aid of his design. There was hardly anything Helen could do that George could not do as well, and some he could do better, while there were many things George was at home in which were sealed to her. The satisfaction of teaching such a pupil he found great. When at length he began to make love to her, Helen found it rather agreeable than otherwise; and, if there was a little more MAKING in it than some women would have liked, Helen was not sufficiently in love with him to detect its presence. Still the pleasure of his preference was such that it opened her mind with a favourable prejudice towards whatever in the shape of theory or doctrine he would have her receive; and much that a more experienced mind would have rejected because of its evident results in practice, was by her accepted in the ignorance which confined her regard of his propositions to their intellectual relations, and prevented her from following them into their influences upon life, which would have reflected light upon their character. For life in its real sense was to her as yet little more definite and present than a dream that waits for the coming night. Hence, when her cousin at length ventured to attack even those doctrines which all women who have received a Christian education would naturally be expected to revere the most, she was able to listen to him unshocked. But she little thought, or he either, that it was only in virtue of what Christian teaching she had had that she was capable of appreciating what was grand in his doctrine of living for posterity without a hope of good result to self beyond the consciousness that future generations of perishing men and women would be a little more comfortable, and perhaps a little less faulty therefrom. She did not reflect, either, that no one's theory concerning death is of much weight in his youth while life FEELS interminable, or that the gift of comfort during a life of so little value that the giver can part with it without regret, is scarcely one to be looked upon as a mighty benefaction.

"But truth is truth," George would have replied.

What you profess to teach them might be a fact, but could never be a truth, I answer. And the veiy value which you falsely put upon facts you have learned to attribute to them from the supposed existence of something at the root of all facts—namely, TRUTHS, or eternal laws of being. Still, if you believe that men will be happier from learning your discovery that there is no

God, preach it, and prosper in proportion to its truth. No; that from my pen would be a curse—no, preach it not, I say, until you have searched all spaces of space, up and down, in greatness and smallness—where I grant indeed, but you cannot know, that you will not find him—and all regions of thought and feeling, all the unknown mental universe of possible discovery—preach it not until you have searched that also, I say, lest what you count a truth should prove to be no fact, and there should after all be somewhere, somehow, a very, living God, a Truth indeed, in whom is the universe. If you say, "But I am convinced there is none," I answer—You may be convinced that there is no God such as this or that in whom men imagine they believe, but you cannot be convinced there is no God.

Meantime George did not forget the present of this life in its future, continued particular about his cigars and his wine, ate his dinners with what some would call a good conscience and I would call a dull one, were I sure it was not a good digestion they really meant, and kept reading hard and to purpose.

Matters as between the two made no rapid advance. George went on loving Helen more than any other woman, and Helen went on liking George next best to her brother Leopold. Whether it came of prudence, of which George possessed not a little, of coldness of temperament, or a pride that would first be sure of acceptance, I do not know, but he made no formal offer yet of handing himself over to Helen, and certainly Helen was in no haste to hear, more than he to utter, the irrevocable.

CHAPTER XIV.

JEREMY TAYLOR.

One Tuesday morning, in the spring, the curate received by the local post the following letter dated from The Park-Gate.

"Respected Sir,

"An obligation on my part which you have no doubt forgotten gives me courage to address you on a matter which seems to me of no small consequence concerning yourself. You do not know me, and the name at the end of my letter will have for you not a single association. The matter itself must be its own excuse.

"I sat in a free seat at the Abbey church last Sunday morning. I had not listened long to the sermon ere I began to fancy I foresaw what was coming, and in a few minutes more I seemed to recognise it as one of Jeremy Taylor's. When I came home, I found that the best portions of one of his sermons had, in the one you read, been wrought up with other material.

"If, sir, I imagined you to be one of such as would willingly have that regarded as their own which was better than they could produce, and would with contentment receive any resulting congratulations, I should feel that I was only doing you a wrong if I gave you a hint which might aid you in avoiding detection; for the sooner the truth concerning such a one was known, and the judgment of society brought to bear upon it, the better for him, whether the result were justification or the contrary. But I have read that in your countenance and demeanour which convinces me that, however custom and the presence of worldly elements in the community to which you belong may have influenced your judgment, you require only to be set thinking of a matter, to follow your conscience with regard to whatever you may find involved in it. I have the honour to be, respected sir,

"Your obedient servant and well-wisher,

"Joseph Polwarth."

Wingfold sat staring at the letter, slightly stunned. The feeling which first grew recognizable in the chaos it had caused, was vexation at having so committed himself; the next, annoyance with his dead old uncle for having led him into such a scrape. There in the good doctor's own handwriting lay the sermon, looking nowise different from the rest! Had he forgotten his marks of quotation? Or to that sermon did he always have a few words of extempore introduction? For himself he was as ignorant of Jeremy Taylor as of Zoroaster. It could not be that that was his uncle's mode of making his sermons? Was it possible they could all be pieces of literary mosaic? It was very annoying. If the fact came to be known, it would certainly be said that he had attempted to pass off Jeremy Taylor's for his own—as if he would have the impudence to make the attempt, and with such a well-known writer! But what difference did it make whether the writer was well or ill known? None, except as to the relative probabilities of escape and discovery! And should the accusation be brought against him, how was he to answer it? By burdening the reputation of his departed uncle with the odium of the fault? Was it worse in his uncle to use Jeremy Taylor than in himself to use his uncle? Or would his remonstrants accept the translocation of blame? Would the church-going or chapel-going inhabitants of Glaston remain mute when it came to be discovered that since his appointment he had not once preached a sermon of his own? How was it that knowing all about it in the background of his mind, he had never come to think of it before? It was true that, admirer of his uncle as he was, he had never imagined himself reaping any laurels from the credit of his sermons; it was equally true however that he had not told a single person of the hidden cistern whence he drew his large discourse. But what could it matter to any man, so long as a good sermon was preached, where it came from? He did not occupy the pulpit in virtue of his personality, but of his office, and it was not a place for the display of originality, but for dispensing the bread of life.—From the stores of other people?—Yes, certainly—if other people's bread was better, and no one the worse for his taking it. "For me, I have none," he said to himself. Why then should that letter have made him uncomfortable? What had he to be ashamed of? Why should he object to being found out? What did he want to conceal? Did not everybody know that very few clergymen really made their own sermons? Was it not absurd, this mute agreement that, although all men knew to the contrary, it must appear to be taken for granted that a man's sermons were of his own mental production? Still more absurd as well as cruel was the way in which they sacrificed to the known falsehood by the contempt they poured upon any fellow the moment they were able to say of productions which never could have been his, that they were by this man or that man, or bought at this shop or that shop in Great Queen Street or Booksellers' Row. After that he was an enduring object for the pointed finger of a mild scorn. It was nothing but the old Spartan game of—steal as you will and enjoy as you can: you are nothing the worse; but woe to you if you are caught in the act! There WAS something contemptible about the whole thing. He was a greater humbug than he had believed himself, for upon this humbug which he now found himself despising he had himself been acting diligently! It dawned upon him that, while there was nothing wrong in preaching his uncle's sermons, there was evil in yielding to cast any veil, even the most transparent, over the fact that the sermons were not his own.

CHAPTER XV

THE PARK GATE.

He had however one considerate, even friendly parishioner, it seemed, whom it became him at least to thank for his openness. He ceased to pace the room, sat down at his writing-table, and acknowledged Mr. Polwarth's letter, expressing his obligation for its contents, and saying that he would do himself the honour of calling upon him that afternoon, in the hope of being allowed to say for himself what little could be said, and of receiving counsel in regard to the difficulty wherein he found himself. He sent the note by his land-lady's boy, and as soon as he had finished his lunch, which meant his dinner, for he could no longer afford to dull his soul in its best time for reading and thinking, he set out to find Park Gate, which he took for some row of dwellings in the suburbs.

Going in the direction pointed out, and finding he had left all the houses behind him, he stopped at the gate of Osterfield Park to make further inquiry. The door of the lodge was opened by one whom he took, for the first half second, to be a child, but recognized the next as the same young woman whose book he had picked up in the fields a few months before. He had never seen her since, but her deformity and her face together had made it easy to remember her.

"We have met before," he said, in answer to her courtesy and smile, "and you must now do me a small favour if you can."

"I shall be most happy, sir. Please come in," she answered.

"I am sorry I cannot at this moment, as I have an engagement. Can you tell me where Mr. Polwarth of the Park Gate lives?"

The girl's smile of sweetness changed to one of amusement as she repeated, in a gentle voice through which ran a thread of suffering,

"Come in, sir, please. My uncle's name is Joseph Polwarth, and this is the gate to Osterfield Park. People know it as the Park-gate."

The house was not one of those trim, modern park-lodges, all angles and peaks, which one sees everywhere now-a-days, but a low cottage, with a very thick, wig-like thatch, into which rose two astonished eyebrows over the stare of two half-awake dormer-windows. On the front of it were young leaves and old hips enough to show that in summer it must be covered with roses.

Wingfold entered at once, and followed her through the kitchen, upon which the door immediately opened, a bright place, with stone floor, and shining things on the walls, to a neat little parlour, cozy and rather dark, with a small window to the garden behind, and a smell of last year's roses.

"My uncle will be here in a few minutes," she said, placing a chair for him. "I would have had a fire here, but my uncle always talks better amongst his books. He expected you, but my lord's steward sent for him up to the new house."

He took the chair she offered him, and sat down to wait. He had not much of the gift of making talk—a questionable accomplishment, —and he never could approach his so-called inferiors but as his equals, the fact being that in their presence he never felt any difference. Notwithstanding his ignorance of the lore of Christianity, Thomas Wingfold was, in regard to some things, gifted with what I am tempted to call a divine stupidity. Many of the distinctions and privileges after which men follow, and of the annoyances and slights over which they fume, were to the curate inappreciable: he did not and could not see them.

"So you are warders of the gate here, Miss Polwarth?" he said, assuming that to be her name, and rightly, when the young woman, who had for a moment left the room, returned.

"Yes," she answered, "we have kept it now for about eight years, sir.—It is no hard task. But I fancy there will be a little more to do when the house is finished."

"It is a long way for you to go to church."

"It would be, sir; but I do not go," she said.

"Your uncle does."

"Not very often, sir."

She left the door open and kept coming and going between the kitchen and the parlour, busy about house affairs. Wingfold sat and watched her as he had opportunity with growing interest.

She had the full-sized head that is so often set on a small body, and it looked yet larger from the quantity of rich brown hair upon it—hair which some ladies would have given their income to possess. Clearly too it gave pleasure to its owner, for it was becomingly as well as carefully and modestly dressed. Her face seemed to Wingfold more interesting every fresh peep he had of it, until at last he pronounced it to himself one of the sweetest he had ever seen. Its prevailing expression was of placidity, and something that was not contentment merely: I would term it satisfaction, were I sure that my reader would call up the very antipode of SELF-satisfaction. And yet there were lines of past and shadows of present suffering upon it. The only sign however that her poor crooked body was not at present totally forgotten, was a slight shy undulation that now and then flickered along the lines of her sensitive mouth, seeming to indicate a shadowy dim-defined thought, or rather feeling, of apology, as if she would disarm prejudice by an expression of sorrow that she could not help the pain and annoyance her unsightliness must occasion. Every feature in her thin face was good, and seemed, individually almost, to speak of a loving spirit, yet he could see ground for suspecting that keen expressions of a quick temper could be no strangers upon those delicately modelled forms. Her hands and feet were both as to size and shape those of a mere child.

He was still studying her like a book which a boy reads by stealth, when with slow step her uncle entered the room.

Wingfold rose and held out his hand.

"You are welcome, sir," said Polwarth, modestly, with the strong grasp of a small firm hand. "Will you walk upstairs with me, where we shall be undisturbed? My niece has, I hope, already made my apologies for not being at home to receive you.—Rachel, my child, will you get us a cup of tea, and by the time it is ready we shall have got through our business, I daresay."

The face of Wingfold's host and new friend in expression a good deal resembled that of his niece, but bore traces of yet greater suffering—bodily, and it might be mental as well. It did not look quite old enough for the whiteness of the plentiful hair that crowned it, and yet there was that in it which might account for the whiteness.

His voice was a little dry and husky, streaked as it were with the asthma whose sounds made that big disproportioned chest seem like the cave of the east wind; but it had a tone of dignity and decision in it, quite in harmony with both matter and style of his letter, and before Wingfold had followed him to the top of the steep narrow straight staircase, all sense of incongruity in him had vanished from his mind.

CHAPTER XVI.

THE ATTIC.

The little man led the way into a tolerably large room, with down-sloping ceiling on both sides, lighted by a small window in the gable, near the fireplace, and a dormer window as well. The low walls, up to the slope, were filled with books; books lay on the table, on the bed, on chairs, and in corners everywhere.

"Aha!" said Wingfold, as he entered and cast his eyes around, "there is no room for surprise that you should have found me out so easily, Mr. Polwarth! Here you have a legion of detectives for such rascals."

The little man turned, and for a moment looked at him with a doubtful and somewhat pained expression, as if he had not been prepared for such an entrance on a solemn question; but a moment's reading of the curate's honest face, which by this time had a good deal more print upon it than would have been found there six months agone, sufficed; the cloud melted into a smile, and he said cordially,

"It is very kind of you, sir, to take my presumption in such good part. Pray sit down, sir. You will find that chair a comfortable one."

"Presumption!" echoed Wingfold. "The presumption was all on my part, and the kindness on yours. But you must first hear my explanation, such as it is. It makes the matter hardly a jot the better, only a man would not willingly look worse, or better either, than he is, and besides, we must understand each other if we would be friends. However unlikely it may seem to you, Mr. Polwarth, I really do share the common weakness of wanting to be taken exactly for what I am, neither more nor less."

"It is a noble weakness, and far enough from common, I am sorry to think," returned Polwarth.

The curate then told the gate-keeper of his uncle's legacy, and his own ignorance of Jeremy Taylor.

"But," he concluded, "since you set me about it, my judgment has capsized itself, and it now seems to me worse to use my uncle's sermons than to have used the bishop's, which anyone might discover to be what they are."

"I see no harm in either," said Polwarth, "provided only it be above board. I believe some clergymen think the only evil lies in detection. I doubt if they ever escape it, and believe the amount of successful deception in that kind to be very small indeed. Many in a congregation can tell, by a kind of instinct, whether a man be preaching his own sermons or not. But the worse evil appears to me to lie in the tacit understanding that a sermon must SEEM to be a man's own, although all in the congregation know, and the would-be preacher knows that they know, that it is none of his."

"Then you mean, Mr. Polwarth, that I should solemnly acquaint my congregation next Sunday with the fact that the sermon I am about to read to them is one of many left me by my worthy uncle, Jonah Driftwood, D.D., who, on his death-bed, expressed the hope that I should support their teaching by my example, for, having gone over them some ten or fifteen times in the course of his incumbency, and bettered each every time until he could do no more for it, he did not think, save by my example, I could carry further the enforcement of the truths they contained:—shall I tell them all that?"

Polwarth laughed, but with a certain seriousness in his merriment, which however took nothing from its genuineness, indeed seemed rather to add thereto.

"It would hardly be needful to enter so fully into particulars," he said. "It would be enough to let them know that you wished it understood between them and you, that you did not profess to teach them anything of yourself, but merely to bring to bear upon them the teaching of others. It would raise complaints and objections, doubtless; but for that you must be prepared if you would do anything right."

Wingfold was silent, thoughtful, saying to himself—"How straight an honest bow can shoot!—But this involves something awful. To stand up in that pulpit and speak about myself! I who, even if I had any opinions, could never see reason for presenting them to other people! It's my office, is it—not me? Then I wish my Office would write his own sermons. He can read the prayers well enough!"

All his life, a little heave of pent-up humour would now and then shake his burden into a more comfortable position upon his bending shoulders. He gave a forlorn laugh.

"But," resumed the small man, "have you never preached a sermon of your own thinking—I don't mean of your own making—one that came out of the commentaries, which are, I am told, the mines whither some of our most noted preachers go to dig for their first inspirations—but one that came out of your own heart—your delight in something you had found out, or something you felt much?"

"No," answered Wingfold; "I have nothing, never had anything worth giving to another; and it would seem to me very unreasonable to subject a helpless congregation to the blundering attempts of such a fellow to put into the forms of reasonable speech things he really knows nothing about."

"You must know about some things which it might do them good to be reminded of—even if they know them already," said Polwarth. "I cannot imagine that a man who looks things in the face as you do, the moment they confront you, has not lived at all, has never met with anything in his history which has taught him something other people need to be taught. I profess myself a believer in preaching, and consider that in so far as the church of England has ceased to be a preaching church—and I don't call nine-tenths of what goes by the name of it PREACHING—she has forgotten a mighty part of her high calling. Of course a man to whom no message has been personally given, has no right to take the place of a prophet—and cannot, save by more or less of simulation—but there is room for teachers as well as prophets, and the more need of teachers that the prophets are so few; and a man may right honestly be a clergyman who teaches the people, though he may possess none of the gifts of prophecy."

"I do not now see well how you are leading me," said Wingfold, considerably astonished at both the aptness and fluency with which a man in his host's position was able to express himself. "Pray, what do you mean by PROPHECY?"

"I mean what I take to be the sense in which St. Paul uses the word—I mean the highest kind of preaching. But I will come to the point practically: a man, I say, who does not feel in his soul that he has something to tell his people, should straightway turn his energy to the providing of such food for them as he finds feed himself. In other words, if he has nothing new in his own treasure, let him bring something old out of another man's. If his own soul is unfed, he can hardly be expected to find food for other people, and has no business in any pulpit, but ought to betake himself to some other employment—whatever he may have been predestined to—I mean, made fit for."

"Then do you intend that a man SHOULD make up his sermons from the books he reads?"

"Yes, if he cannot do better. But then I would have him read—not with his sermon in his eye, but with his people in his heart. Men in business and professions have so little time for reading or thinking—and idle people have still less—that their means of grace, as the theologians say, are confined to discipline without nourishment, whence their religion, if they have any, is often from mere atrophy but a skeleton; and the office of preaching is, after all, to wake them up lest their sleep turn to death; next, to make them hungry, and lastly, to supply that hunger; and for all these things, the pastor has to take thought. If he feed not the flock of God, then is he an hireling and no shepherd."

At this moment, Rachel entered with a small tea-tray: she could carry only little things, and a few at a time. She cast a glance of almost loving solicitude at the young man who now sat before her uncle with head bowed, and self-abasement on his honest countenance, then a look almost of expostulation at her uncle, as if interceding for a culprit, and begging the master not to be too hard upon him. But the little man smiled—such a sweet smile of re-assurance, that her face returned at once to its prevailing expression of content. She cleared a place on the table, set down her tray, and went to bring cups and saucers.

CHAPTER XVII.

POLWARTH'S PLAN.

"I think I understand you now," said Wingfold, after the little pause occasioned by the young woman's entrance. "You would have a man who cannot be original, deal honestly in second-hand goods. Or perhaps rather, he should say to the congregation—'This is not home-made bread I offer you, but something better. I got it from this or that baker's shop. I have eaten of it myself, and it has agreed well with me and done me good. If you chew it well, I don't doubt you also will find it good.'—Is that something like what you would have, Mr. Polwarth?"

"Precisely," answered the gate-keeper. "But," he added, after a moment's delay, "I should be sorry if you stopped there."

"Stopped there!" echoed Wingfold. "The question is whether I can begin there. You have no idea how ignorant I am—how little I have read!"

"I have some idea of both, I fancy. I must have known considerably less than you at your age, for I was never at a university."

"But perhaps even then you had more of the knowledge which, they say, life only can give."

"I have it now at all events. But of that everyone has enough who lives his life. Those who gain no experience are those who shirk the king's highway, for fear of encountering the Duty seated by the roadside."

"You ought to be a clergyman yourself, sir," said Wingfold, humbly. "How is it that such as I——"

Here he checked himself, knowing something of how it was.

"I hope I ought to be just what I am, neither more nor less," replied Polwarth. "As to being a clergyman, Moses had a better idea about such things, at least so far as concerns outsides, than you seem to have, Mr. Wingfold. He would never have let a man who in size and shape is a mere mockery of the human, stand up to minister to the congregation. But if you will let me help you, I shall be most grateful; for of late I have been oppressed with the thought that I serve no one but myself and my niece. I am in mortal fear of growing selfish under the weight of my privileges."

A fit of asthmatic coughing seized him, and grew in severity until he seemed struggling for his life. It was at the worst when his niece entered, but she showed no alarm, only concern, and did nothing but go up to him and lay her hand on his back between his shoulders till the fit was over. The instant the convulsion ceased, its pain dissolved in a smile.

Wingfold uttered some lame expressions of regret that he should suffer so much.

"It is really nothing to distress you, or me either, Mr. Wingfold," said the little man. "Shall we have a cup of tea, and then resume our talk?"

"The fact, I find, Mr. Polwarth," said the curate, giving the result of what had been passing through his mind, and too absorbed in that to reply to the invitation, "is, that I must not, and indeed cannot give you half-confidences. I will tell you all that troubles me, for it is plain that you know something of which I am ignorant, —something which, I have great hopes, will turn out to be the very thing I need to know. May I speak? Will you let me talk about myself?"

"I am entirely at your service, Mr. Wingfold," returned Polwarth, and seeing the curate did not touch his tea, placed his own cup again on the table.

The young woman got down like a child from the chair upon which she had perched herself at the table, and with a kind look at Wingfold, was about to leave the room.

"No, no, Miss Polwarth!" said the curate, rising; "I shall not be able to go on if I feel that I have sent you away—and your tea untouched too! What a selfish and ungrateful fellow I am! I did not even observe that you had given me tea! But you would pardon me if you knew what I have been going through. If you don't mind staying, we can talk and drink our tea at the same time. I am very fond of tea, when it is so good as I see yours is. I only fear I may have to say some things that will shock you."

"I will stay till then," replied Rachel, with a smile, and climbed again upon her chair. "I am not much afraid. My uncle says things sometimes fit to make a Pharisee's hair stand on his head, but somehow they make my heart burn inside me.—May I stop, uncle?—I should like so much!"

"Certainly, my child, if Mr. Wingfold will not feel your presence a restraint."

"Not in the least," said the curate.

Miss Polwarth helped them to bread and butter, and a brief silence followed.

"I was brought up to the church," said Wingfold at length, playing with his teaspoon, and looking down on the table. "It's an awful shame such a thing should have been, but I don't find out that anybody in particular was to blame for it. Things are all wrong that way, in general, I doubt. I pass my examinations with decency, distinguish myself in nothing, go before the bishop, am admitted a deacon, after a year am ordained a priest, and after another year or two of false preaching and of parish work, suddenly find myself curate in charge of a grand old abbey church; but as to what the whole thing means in practical relation with myself as a human being, I am as ignorant as Simon Magus, without his excuse. Do not mistake me. I think I could stand an examination on the doctrines of the church, as contained in the articles, and prayer-book generally. But for all they have done for me, I might as well have never heard of them."

"Don't be quite sure of that, Mr. Wingfold. At least, they have brought you to inquire if there be anything in them."

"Mr. Polwarth," returned Wingfold abruptly, "I cannot even prove there is a God!"

"But the church of England exists for the sake of teaching Christianity, not proving that there is a God."

"What is Christianity, then?"

"God in Christ, and Christ in man."

"What is the use of that if there be no God?"

"None whatever."

"Mr. Polwarth, can you prove there is a God?"

"No."

"Then if you don't believe there is a God—I don't know what is to become of me," said the curate, in a tone of deep disappointment, and rose to go.

"Mr. Wingfold," said the little man, with a smile and a deep breath as of delight at the thought that was moving in him, "I know him in my heart, and he is all in all to me. You did not ask whether I believed in him, but whether I could prove that there was a God. As well ask a fly, which has not yet crawled about the world, if he can prove that it is round!"

"Pardon me, and have patience with me," said Wingfold, resuming his seat. "I am a fool. But it is life or death to me."

"I would we were all such fools!—But please ask me no more questions; or ask me as many as you will, but expect no answers just yet. I want to know more of your mind first."

"Well, I will ask questions, but press for no answers.—If you cannot prove there is a God, do you know for certain that such a one as Jesus Christ ever lived? Can it be proved with positive certainty? I say nothing of what they call the doctrines of Christianity, or the authority of the church, or the sacraments, or anything of that sort. Such questions are at present of no interest to me. And yet the fact that they do not interest me, were enough to prove me in as false and despicable a position as ever man found himself occupying—as arrant a hypocrite and deceiver as any god-personating priest in the Delphic temple.—I had rather a man despised than excused me, Mr. Polwarth, for I am at issue with myself, and love not my past."

"I shall do neither, Mr. Wingfold. Go on, if you please, sir. I am more deeply interested than I can tell you."

"Some few months ago then, I met a young man who takes for granted the opposite of all that I had up to that time taken for granted, and which now I want to be able to prove. He spoke with contempt of my profession. I could not defend my profession, and of course had to despise myself. I began to think. I began to pray—if you will excuse me for mentioning it. My whole past life appeared like the figures that glide over the field of a camera obscura—not an abiding fact in it all. A cloud gathered about me, and hangs about me still. I call, but no voice answers me out of the darkness, and at times I am in despair. I would, for the love and peace of honesty, give up the profession, but I shrink from forsaking what I may yet possibly find—though I fear, I fear—to be as true as I wish to find it. Something, I know not what, holds me to it—some dim vague affection, possibly mere prejudice, aided by a love for music, and the other sweet sounds of our prayers and responses. Nor would I willingly be supposed to deny what I dare not say—indeed know not how to say I believe, not knowing what it is. I should nevertheless have abandoned everything months ago, had I not felt bound by my agreement to serve my rector for a year. You are the only one of the congregation who has shown me any humanity, and I beg of you to be my friend and help me. What shall I do? After the avowal you have made, I may well ask you again, How am I to know that there is a God?"

"It were a more pertinent question, sir," returned Polwarth,—"If there be a God, how am I to find him?—And, as I hinted before, there is another question—one you have already put—more pertinent to your position as an English clergyman: Was there ever such a man as Jesus Christ?—Those, I think, were your own words: what do you mean by SUCH a man?"

"Such as he is represented in the New Testament."

"From that representation, what description would you give of him now? What is that SUCH? What sort of person, supposing the story true, would you take this Jesus, from that story, to have been?"

Wingfold thought for a while.

"I am a worse humbug than I fancied," he said. "I cannot tell what he was. My thoughts of him are so vague and indistinct that it would take me a long time to render myself able to answer your question."

"Perhaps longer still than you think, sir. It took me a very long time.—"

CHAPTER XVIII.

JOSEPH POLWARTH.

"Shall I tell you," the gate-keeper went on, "something of my life, in return of the confidence you have honoured me with?"

"Nothing could be more to my mind," answered Wingfold. "And I trust," he added, "it is no unworthy curiosity that makes me anxious to understand how you have come to know so much."

"Indeed it is not that I know much," said the little man. "On the contrary I am the most ignorant person of my acquaintance. You would be astonished to discover what I don't know. But the thing is that I know what is worth knowing. Yet I get not a crumb more than my daily bread by it—I mean the bread by which the inner man lives. The man who gives himself to making money, will seldom fail of becoming a rich man; and it would be hard if a man who gave himself to find wherewithal to still the deepest cravings of his best self, should not be able to find that bread of life. I tried to make a little money by book-selling once: I failed—not to pay my debts, but to make the money; I could not go into it heartily, or give it thought enough, so it was all right I should not succeed; but what I did and do make my object, does not disappoint me.

"My ancestors, as my name indicates, were of and in Cornwall, where they held large property. Forgive the seeming boast—it is but fact, and can reflect little enough on one like me. Scorn and pain mingled with mighty hope is a grand prescription for weaning the heart from the judgments and aspirations of this world. Later ancestors were, not many generations ago, the proprietors of this very property of Osterfield, which the uncle of the present Lord de Barre bought, and to which I, their descendant, am gate-keeper. What with gambling, drinking, and worse, they deserved to lose it. The results of their lawlessness are ours: we are what and where you see us. With the inherited poison, the Father gave the antidote. Rachel, my child, am I not right when I say that you thank God with me for having THUS visited the iniquities of the fathers upon the children?"

"I do, uncle; you know I do—from the bottom of my heart," replied Rachel in a low tender voice.

A great solemnity came upon the spirit of Wingfold, and for a moment he felt as if he sat wrapt in a cloud of sacred marvel, beyond and around which lay a gulf of music too perfect to touch his sense. But presently Polwarth resumed:

"My father was in appearance a remarkably fine man, tall and stately. Of him I have little to say. If he did not do well, my grandfather must be censured first. He had a sister very like Rachel here. Poor Aunt Lottie! She was not so happy as my little one. My brothers were all fine men like himself, yet they all died young except my brother Robert. He too is dead now, thank God, and I trust he is in peace. I had almost begun to fear with himself that he would never die. And yet he was but fifty. He left me my Rachel with her twenty pounds a year. I have thirty of my own, and this cottage we have rent-free for attending to the gate. I shall tell you more about my brother some day. There are none of the family left now but myself and Rachel. God in his mercy is about to let it cease.

"I was sent to one of our smaller public schools—mainly, I believe, because I was an eyesore to my handsome father. There I made, I fancy, about as good a beginning as wretched health, and the miseries of a sensitive nature, ever conscious of exposure, without mother or home to hide its feebleness and deformity, would permit. For then first I felt myself an outcast. I was the butt of all the coarser-minded of my schoolfellows, and the kindness of some could but partially make up for it. On the other hand, I had no haunting and irritating sense of wrong, such as I believe not a few of my fellows in deformity feel—no burning indignation, or fierce impulse to retaliate on those who injured me, or on the society that scorned me. The isolation that belonged to my condition wrought indeed to the intensifying of my individuality, but that again intensified my consciousness of need more than of wrong, until the passion blossomed almost into assurance, and at length I sought even with agony the aid to which my wretchedness seemed to have a right. My longing was mainly for a refuge, for some corner into which I might creep, where I should be concealed and so at rest. The sole triumph I coveted over my persecutors was to know that they could not find me—that I had a friend stronger than they. It is no wonder I should not remember when I began to pray, and hope that God heard me. I used to fancy to myself that I lay in his hand and peeped through his fingers at my foes. That was at night, for my deformity brought me one blessed comfort—that I had no bedfellow. This I felt at first as both a sad deprivation and a painful rejection, but I learned to pray the sooner for the loneliness, and the heartier from the solitude which was as a chamber with closed door.

"I do not know what I might have taken to had I been made like other people, or what plans my mother cherished for me. But it soon became evident, as time passed and I grew no taller but more mis-shapen, that to bring me up to a profession would be but to render my deformity the more painful to myself. I spent, therefore, the first three years after I left school at home, keeping out of my father's way as much as possible, and cleaving fast to my mother. When she died, she left her little property between me and my brother. He had been brought up to my father's profession—that of an engineer. My father could not touch the principal of this money, but neither, while he lived, could we the interest. I hardly know how I lived for the next three or four years—it must have been almost on charity, I think. My father was never at home, and but for the old woman who had been our only attendant all my life, I think very likely I should have starved. I spent my time mostly in reading—whatever I could lay my hands upon—and that not carelessly, but with such reflection as I was capable of. One thing I may mention, as showing how I was still carried in the same direction as before—that, without any natural turn for handicraft, I constructed for myself a secret place of carpenter's work in a corner of the garret, small indeed, but big enough for a couch on which I could lie, and a table as long as the couch. That was all the furniture. The walls were lined from top to bottom with books, mostly gathered from those lying about the house. Cunningly was the entrance to this nest contrived: I doubt if anyone may have found it yet. If some imaginative, dreamy boy has come upon it, what a find it must have been to him! I could envy him the pleasure. There I always went to say my prayers and read my bible. But sometimes The Arabian Nights, or some other book of entrancing human invention, would come between, and make me neglect both, and then I would feel bad and forsaken;—for as yet I knew little of the heart to which I cried for shelter and warmth and defence.

"Somewhere in this time at length, I began to feel dissatisfied, even displeased with myself. At first the feeling was vague, altogether undefined—a mere sense that I did not fit into things, that I was not what I ought to be, what was somehow and by the Authority required of me. This went on, began to gather roots rather than send them out, grew towards something more definite. I began to be aware that, heavy affliction as it was to be made so different from my fellows, my outward deformity was but a picture of my inward condition. There nothing was right. Many things which in theory I condemned, and in others despised, were yet a part of myself, or, at best, part of evil disease cleaving fast unto me. I found myself envious and revengeful and conceited. I discovered that I looked down on people whom I thought less clever than myself. Once I caught myself scorning a young fellow to whose disadvantage I knew nothing, except that God had made him handsome enough for a woman. All at once one day, with a sickening conviction it came upon me—with one of those sudden slackenings of the cord of self-consciousness, in which it doubles back quivering, and seems to break, while the man for an instant beholds his individuality apart from himself, is generally frightened at it, and always disgusted—a strange and indeed awful experience, which if it lasted longer than its allotted moment, might well drive a man mad who had no God to whom to offer back his individuality, in appeal against his double consciousness—it was in one of these cataleptic fits of the spirit, I say, that I first saw plainly what a contemptible little wretch I was, and writhed in the bright agony of conscious worthlessness.

"I now concluded that I had been nothing but a pharisee and a hypocrite, praying with a bad heart, and that God saw me just as detestable as I saw myself, and despised me and was angry with me. I read my bible more diligently than ever for a time, found in it nothing but denunciation and wrath, and soon dropped it in despair. I had already ceased to pray.

"One day a little boy mocked me. I flew into a rage, and, rendered by passion for the moment fleet and strong, pursued and caught him. Whatever may be a man's condition of defence against evil, I have learnt that he cannot keep the good out of him. When the boy found himself in my clutches, he turned on me a look of such terror that it disarmed me at once, and, confounded and distressed to see a human being in such abject fear, a state which in my own experience I knew to be horrible, ashamed also that it should be before such a one as myself, I would have let him go instantly, but that I could not without first having comforted him. But not a word of mine could get into his ears, and I saw at length that he was so PRE-possessed, that every tone of kindness I uttered, sounded to him a threat: nothing would do but let him go. The moment he found himself free, he fled headlong into the pond, got out again, ran home, and told, with perfect truthfulness I believe, though absolute inaccuracy, that I threw him in. After this I tried to govern my temper, but found that the more I tried, the more even that I succeeded outwardly, that is, succeeded in suppressing the signs and deeds of wrath, the less could I keep down the wrath in my soul. I then tried never to think about myself at all, and read and read—not the bible—more and more, in order to forget myself. But ever through all my reading and thinking I was aware of the lack of harmony at the heart of me: I was not that which it was well to be; I was not at peace; I lacked; was distorted; I was sick. Such were my feelings, not my reflections. All that time is as the memory of an unlovely dream—a dream of confusion and pain.

"One evening, in the twilight, I lay alone in my little den, not thinking, but with mind surrendered and passive to what might come into it. It was very hot—indeed sultry. My little skylight was open, but not a breath of air entered. What preceded I do not know, but the face of the terrified boy rose before me, or in me rather, and all at once I found myself eagerly, painfully, at length almost in an agony, persuading him that I would not hurt him, but meant well and friendlily towards him. Again I had just let him go in despair, when the sweetest, gentlest, most refreshing little waft of air came in at the window and just went BEING, hardly moving, over my forehead. Its greeting was more delicate than even my mother's kiss, and yet it cooled my whole body. Now whatever, or whencesoever the link, if any be supposed needful to account for the fact, it kept below in the secret places of the springs, for I saw it not; but the next thought of which I was aware was—What if I misunderstood God the same way the boy had misunderstood me! and the next thing was to take my New Testament from the shelf on which I had laid it aside.

"Another evening of that same summer, I said to myself that I would begin at the beginning and read it through. I had no definite idea in the resolve; it seemed a good thing to do, and I would do it. It would serve towards keeping up my connection in a way with THINGS ABOVE. I began, but did not that night get through the first chapter of St. Matthew. Conscientiously I read every word of the genealogy, but when I came to the twenty-third verse and read: 'Thou shalt call his name Jesus; FOR HE SHALL SAVE HIS PEOPLE FROM THEIR SINS,' I fell on my knees. No system of theology had come between me and a common-sense reading of the book. I did not for a moment imagine that to be saved from my sins meant to be saved from the punishment of them. That would have been no glad tidings to me. My sinfulness was ever before me, and often my sins too, and I loved them not, yet could not free myself of them. They were in me and of me, and how was I to part myself from that which came to me with my consciousness, which asserted itself in me as one with my consciousness? I could not get behind myself so as to reach its root. But here was news of one who came from behind that root itself to deliver me from that in me which made being a bad thing! Ah, Mr. Wingfold! what if, after all the discoveries made, and all the theories set up and pulled down, amid all the commonplaces men call common sense, notwithstanding all the over-powering and excluding self-assertion of things that are seen, ever crying, 'Here we are, and save us there is nothing: the Unseen is the Unreal!'—what if, I say, notwithstanding all this, it should yet be that the strongest weapon a man can wield is prayer to one who made him! What if the man who lifts up his heart to the unknown God even, be entering, amid the mockery of men who worship what they call natural law and science, into the region whence issues every law, and where the very material of science is born!

"To tell you all that followed, if I could recall and narrate it in order, would take hours. Suffice it that from that moment I was a student, a disciple. Soon to me also came then the two questions: HOW DO I KNOW THAT THERE IS A GOD AT ALL? and—HOW AM I TO KNOW THAT SUCH A MAN AS JESUS EVERY LIVED? I could answer neither. But in the meantime I was reading the story—was drawn to the man there presented—and was trying to understand his being, and character, and principles of life and action. And, to sum all in a word, many months had not passed ere I had forgotten to seek an answer to either question: they were in fact questions no longer: I had seen the man Christ Jesus, and in him had known the Father of him and of me. My dear sir, no conviction can be got, or if it could be got, would be of any sufficing value, through that dealer in second-hand goods, the intellect. If by it we could prove there is a God, it would be of small avail indeed: we must see him and know him, to know that he was not a demon. But I know no other way of knowing that there is a God but that which reveals WHAT he is—the only idea that could be God—shows him in his own self-proving existence—and that way is Jesus Christ as he revealed himself on earth, and as he is revealed afresh to every heart that seeks to know the truth concerning him."

A pause followed, a solemn one, and then again Polwarth spoke:

"Either the whole frame of existence," he said, "is a wretched, miserable unfitness, a chaos with dreams of a world, a chaos in which the higher is for ever subject to the lower, or it is an embodied idea growing towards perfection in him who is the one perfect creative Idea, the Father of lights, who suffers himself that he may bring his many sons into the glory which is his own glory."

CHAPTER XIX.

THE CONCLUSION OF THE WHOLE MATTER.

"But," said Wingfold—"only pray do not think I am opposing you; I am in the straits you have left so far behind: how am I to know that I should not merely have wrought myself up to the believing of that which I should like to be true?"

"Leave that question, my dear sir, until you know what that really is which you want to believe. I do not imagine that you have more than the merest glimmer of the nature of that concerning which you, for the very reason that you know not what it is, most rationally doubt. Is a man to refuse to withdraw his curtains lest some flash in his own eyes should deceive him with a vision of morning while yet it is night? The truth to the soul is as light to the eyes: you may be deceived, and mistake something else for light, but you can never fail to know the light when it really comes."

"What then would you have of me?—what am I to DO?" said Wingfold, who, having found his master, was docile as a child, but had not laid firm enough hold upon what he had last said.

"I repeat," said Polwarth, "that the community whose servant you are was not founded to promulgate or defend the doctrine of the existence of a Deity, but to perpetuate the assertion of a man that he was the son and only revealer of the Father of men, a fact, if it be a fact, which precludes the question of the existence of a God, because it includes the answer to it. Your business, therefore, even as one who finds himself in your unfortunate position as a clergyman, is to make yourself acquainted with that man: he will be to you nobody save in revealing, through knowledge of his inmost heart, the Father to you. Take then your New Testament as if you had never seen it before, and read—to find out. If in him you fail to meet God, then go to your consciousness of the race, your metaphysics, your Plato, your Spinosa. Till then, this point remains: there was a man who said he knew him, and that if you would give heed to him, you too should know him. The record left of him is indeed scanty, yet enough to disclose what manner of man he was—his principles, his ways of looking at things, his thoughts of his Father and his brethren and the relations between them, of man's business in life, his destiny, and his hopes."

"I see plainly," answered the curate, "that what you say, I must do. But how, while on duty as a clergyman, I DO NOT KNOW. How am I, with the sense of the unreality of my position ever growing upon me, and my utter inability to supply the wants of the congregation, save from my uncle's store of dry provender, which it takes me a great part of my time so to modify as, in using it, to avoid direct lying—with all this pressing upon me, and making me restless and irritable and self-contemptuous, how AM I to set myself to such solemn work, wherein a man must surely be clear-eyed and single-hearted, if he would succeed in his quest?—I must resign my curacy."

Mr. Polwarth thought a little.

"It would be well, I think, to retain it for a time at least while you search," he said. "If you do not within a month see prospect of finding him, then resign. In any case, your continuance in the service must depend on your knowledge of the lord of it, and his will concerning you."

"May not a prejudice in favour of my profession blind and deceive me?"

"I think it will rather make YOU doubtful of conclusions that support it."

"I will go and try," said Wingfold, rising; "but I fear I am not the man to make discoveries in such high regions."

"You are the man to find what fits your own need if the thing be there," said Polwarth. "But to ease your mind for the task: I know pretty well some of our best English writers of the more practical and poetic sort in theology— the two qualities go together—and if you will do me the favour to come again to-morrow, I shall be able, I trust, to provide you wherewithal to feed your flock, free of that duplicity which, be it as common as the surplice, and as fully connived as laughed at by that flock, is yet duplicity. There is no law that sermons shall be the preacher's own, but there is an eternal law against all manner of humbug. Pardon the word."

"I will not attempt to thank you," said Wingfold, "but I will do as you tell me. You are the first real friend I have ever had—except my brother, who is dead."

"Perhaps you have had more friends than you are aware of. You owe something to the man, for instance, who, with his outspoken antagonism, roused you first to a sense of what was lacking to you."

"I hope I shall be grateful to God for it some day," returned Wingfold. "I cannot say that I feel much obligation to Mr. Bascombe. And yet when I think of it,—perhaps—I don't know—what ought a man to be more grateful for than honesty?"

After a word of arrangement for next day the curate took his leave, assuredly with a stronger feeling of simple genuine respect than he had ever yet felt for man. Rachel bade him good night with her fine eyes filled with tears, which suited their expression, for they always seemed to be looking through sorrow to something beyond it.

"If this be a type of the way the sins of the fathers are visited upon the children," said the curate to himself, "there must be more in the progression of history than political economy can explain. It would drive us to believe in an economy wherein rather the well-being of the whole was the result of individual treatment, and not the well-being of the individual the result of the management of the whole?"

I will not count the milestones along the road on which Wingfold now began to journey. Some of the stages, however, will appear in the course of my story. When he came to any stiff bit of collar-work, the little man generally appeared with an extra horse. Every day during the rest of that week he saw his new friends.

CHAPTER XX.

A STRANGE SERMON.

On the Sunday the curate walked across the churchyard to the morning prayer very much as if the bells, instead of ringing the people to church, had been tolling for his execution. But if he was going to be hanged, he would at least die like a gentleman, confessing his sin. Only he would it were bed-time, and all well. He trembled so when he stood up to read that he could not tell whether or not he was speaking in a voice audible to the congregation. But as his hour drew near, the courage to meet it drew near also, and when at length he ascended the pulpit stairs, he was able to cast a glance across the sea of heads to learn whether the little man was in the poor seats. But he looked for the big head in vain.

When he read his text, it was to a congregation as listless and indifferent as it was wont to be. He had not gone far, however, before that change of mental condition was visible in the faces before him, which a troop of horses would have shown by a general forward swivelling of the ears. Wonderful to tell, they were actually listening. But in truth it was no wonder, for seldom in any, and assuredly never in that church, had there been heard such an exordium to a sermon.

His text was—"Confessing your faults one to another." Having read it with a return of the former trembling, and paused, his brain suddenly seemed for a moment to reel under a wave of extinction that struck it, then to float away upon it, and then to dissolve in it, as it interpenetrated its whole mass, annihilating thought and utterance together. But with a mighty effort of the will, in which he seemed to come as near as man could come to the willing of his own existence, he recovered himself and went on. To do justice to this effort, my reader must remember that he was a shy man, and that he knew his congregation but too well for an unsympathetic one—whether from their fault or his own mattered little for the nonce. It had been hard enough to make up his mind to the attempt when alone in his study, or rather, to tell the truth, in his chamber, but to carry out his resolve in the face of so many faces, and in spite of a cowardly brain, was an effort and a victory indeed. Yet after all, upon second thoughts, I see that the true resolve was the victory, sweeping shyness and every other opposing weakness along with it. But it wanted courage of yet another sort to make of his resolve a fact, and his courage, in that kind as well, had never yet been put to the test or trained by trial. He had not been a fighting boy at school; he had never had the chance of riding to hounds; he had never been in a shipwreck, or a house on fire; had never been waked from a sound sleep with a demand for his watch and money; yet one who had passed creditably through all these trials, might still have carried a doubting conscience to his grave rather than face what Wingfold now confronted.

From the manuscript before him he read thus:

"'Confess your faults one to another.'—This command of the apostle, my hearers, ought to justify me in doing what I fear some of you may consider almost as a breach of morals—talking of myself in the pulpit. But in the pulpit has a wrong been done, and in the pulpit shall it be confessed. From Sunday to Sunday, standing on this spot, I have read to you, without word of explanation, as if they formed the message I had sought and found for you, the thoughts and words of another. Doubtless they were better than any I could have given you from my own mind or experience, and the act had been a righteous one, had I told you the truth concerning them. But that truth I did not tell you.—At last, through words of honest expostulation, the voice of a friend whose wounds are faithful, I have been aroused to a knowledge of the wrong I have been doing. Therefore I now confess it. I am sorry. I will do so no more.

"But, brethren, I have only a little garden on a bare hill-side, and it hath never yet borne me any fruit fit to offer for your acceptance; also, my heart is troubled about many things, and God hath humbled me. I beg of you, therefore, to bear with me for a little while, if, doing what is but lawful and expedient both, I break through the bonds of custom in order to provide you with food convenient for you. Should I fail in this, I shall make room for a better man. But for your bread of this day, I go gleaning openly in other men's fields—fields into which I could not have found my way, in time at least for your necessities, and where I could not have gathered such full ears of wheat, barley, and oats but for the more than assistance of the same friend who warned me of the wrong I was doing both you and myself. Right ancient fields are some of them, where yet the ears lie thick for the gleaner. To continue my metaphor: I will lay each handful before you with the name of the field where I gathered it; and together they will serve to show what some of the wisest and best shepherds of the English flock have believed concerning the duty of confessing our faults." He then proceeded to read the extracts which Mr. Polwarth had helped him to find—and arrange, not chronologically, but after an idea of growth. Each handful, as he called it, he prefaced with one or two words concerning him in whose field he had gleaned it.

His voice steadied and strengthened as he read. Renewed contact with the minds of those vanished teachers gave him a delight which infused itself into the uttered words, and made them also joyful; and if the curate preached to no one else in the congregation, certainly he preached to himself, and before it was done had entered into a thorough enjoyment of the sermon.

A few in the congregation were disappointed because they had looked for a justification and enforcement of the confessional, thinking the change in the curate could only have come from that portion of the ecclesiastical heavens towards which they themselves turned their faces. A few others were scandalized at such an innovation on the part of a young man who was only a curate. Many however declared that it was the most interesting sermon they had ever heard in their lives—which perhaps was not saying much.

Mrs. Ramshorn made a class by herself. Not having yet learned to like Wingfold, and being herself one of the craft, with a knowledge of not a few of the secrets of the clerical—prison-house, shall I call it, or green-room?—she was indignant with the presumptuous young man who degraded the pulpit to a level with the dock. Who cared for him? What was it to a congregation of respectable people, many of them belonging to the first county families, that he, a mere curate, should have committed what he fancied a crime against them! He should have waited until it had been laid to his charge. Couldn't he repent of his sins, whatever they were, without making a boast of them in the pulpit, and exposing them to the eyes of a whole congregation? She had known people make a stock-in-trade of their sins! What was it to them whether the washy stuff he gave them by way of sermons was his own foolishness or some other noodle's! Nobody would have troubled himself to inquire into his honesty, if he had but held his foolish tongue. Better men than he had preached other people's sermons and never thought it worth mentioning. And what worse were the people? The only harm lay in letting them know it; that brought the profession into disgrace, and prevented the good the sermon would otherwise have done, besides giving the enemies of the truth a handle against the church. And then such a thing to call a sermon! As well take a string of blown eggs to market! Thus she expatiated, half the way home, before either of her companions found an opportunity of saying a word.

"I am sorry to differ from you, aunt," said Helen. "I thought the sermon a very interesting one. He read beautifully."

"For my part," said Bascombe, who was now a regular visitor from Saturdays to Mondays, "I used to think the fellow a muff, but, by Jove! I've changed my mind. If ever there was a plucky thing to do, that was one, and there ain't many men, let me tell you, aunt, who would have the pluck for it.—It's my belief, Helen," he went on, turning to her and speaking in a lower tone, "I've had the honour of doing that fellow some good. I gave him my mind about honesty pretty plainly the first time I saw him. And who can tell what may come next when a fellow once starts in the right way! We shall have him with us before long. I must look out for something for him, for of course he'll be in a devil of a fix without his profession."

"I am so glad you think with me, George!" said Helen. "There was always something I was inclined to like about Mr. Wingfold. Indeed I should have liked him quite if he had not been so painfully modest."

"Notwithstanding his sheepishness, though," returned Bascombe, "there was a sort of quiet self-satisfaction about him, and the way he always said Don't you think? as if he were Socrates taking advantage of Mr. Green and softly guiding him into a trap, which I confess made me set him down as conceited; but, as I say, I begin to change my mind. By Jove! he must have worked pretty hard too in the dust-bins to get together all those bits of gay rag and resplendent crockery!"

"You heard him say he had help," said Helen.

"No, I don't remember that."

"It came just after that pretty simile about gleaning in old fields."

"I remember the simile, for I thought it a very absurd one—as if fields would lie gleanable for generations!"

"To be sure—now you point it out!" acquiesced Helen.

"The grain would have sprouted and borne harvests a hundred. If a man will use figures, he should be careful to give them legs. I wonder whom he got to help him—not the rector, I suppose?"

"The rector!" echoed Mrs. Ramshorn, who had been listening to the young people's remarks with a smile of quiet scorn on her lip, thinking what an advantage was experience, even if it could not make up for the loss of youth and beauty—"The last man in the world to lend himself to such a miserable makeshift and pretence! Without brains enough even to fancy himself able to write a sermon of his own, he flies to the dead,—to their very coffins as it were—and I will not say STEALS from them, for he does it openly, not having even shame enough to conceal his shame!"

"I like a man to hold his face to what he does, or thinks either," said Bascombe.

"Ah, George!" returned his aunt, in tones of wisdom, "by the time you have had my experience, you will have learned a little prudence."

Meantime, so far as his aunt was concerned, George did use prudence, for in her presence he did not hold his face to what he thought. He said to himself it would do her no good. She was so prejudiced! and it might interfere with his visits.—She, for her part, never had the slightest doubt of his orthodoxy: was he not the son of a clergyman and canon?—a grandson of the church herself?

CHAPTER XXI.

A THUNDERBOLT.

Sometimes a thunderbolt, as men call it, will shoot from a clear sky; and sometimes into the midst of a peaceful family, or a yet quieter individuality, without warning of gathered storm above, or lightest tremble of earthquake beneath, will fall a terrible fact, and from the moment everything is changed. That family or that life is no more what it was—probably never more can be what it was. Better it ought to be, worse it may be—which, depends upon itself. But its spiritual weather is altered. The air is thick with cloud, and cannot weep itself clear. There may come a gorgeous sunset though.

It were a truism for one who believes in God to say that such catastrophes, so rending, so frightful, never come but where they are needed. The Power of Life is not content that they who live in and by him should live poorly and contemptibly. If the presence of low thoughts which he repudiates, yet makes a man miserable, how must it be with him if they who live and move and have their being in him are mean and repulsive, or alienated through self-sufficiency and slowness of heart?

I cannot report much progress in Helen during the months of winter and spring. But if one wakes at last, wakes at all, who shall dare cast the stone at him—that he ought to have awaked sooner? What man who is awake will dare to say that he roused himself the first moment it became possible to him? The main and plain and worst, perhaps only condemnation is—that when people do wake they do not get up. At the same time, however, I can hardly doubt that Helen was keeping the law of a progress slow as the growth of an iron-tree.

Nothing had ever yet troubled her. She had never been in love, could hardly be said to be in love now. She went regularly to church, and I believe said her prayers night and morning—yet felt no indignation at the doctrines and theories propounded by George Bascombe. She regarded them as "George's ideas," and never cared to ask whether they were true or not, at the same time that they were becoming to her by degrees as like truth as falsehood can ever be. For to the untruthful mind the false CAN seem the true. Meantime she was not even capable of giving him the credit he deserved, in that, holding the opinions he held, he yet advocated a life spent for the community—without, as I presume, deriving much inspiration thereto from what he himself would represent as the ground of all conscientious action, the consideration, namely, of its reaction upon its originator. Still farther was it from entering the field of her vision that possibly some of the good which distinguished George's unbelief from that of his brother ephemera of the last century, was owing to the deeper working of that leaven which he denounced as the poisonous root whence sprung all the evil diseases that gnawed at the heart of society.

One night she sat late, making her aunt a cap. The one sign of originality in her was the character of her millinery, of which kind of creation she was fond, displaying therein both invention as to form, and perception as to effect, combined with lightness and deftness of execution. She was desirous of completing it before the next morning, which was that of her aunt's birthday. They had had friends to dine with them who had stayed rather late, and it was now getting towards one o'clock. But Helen was not easily tired, and was not given to abandoning what she had undertaken; so she sat working away, and thinking, not of George Bascombe, but of one whom she loved better—far better—her brother Leopold. But she was thinking of him not quite so comfortably as usual. Certain anxieties she had ground for concerning him had grown stronger, for the time since she heard from him had grown very long.

All at once her work ceased, her hands were arrested, her posture grew rigid: she was listening. HAD she heard a noise outside her window? My reader may remember that it opened on a balcony, which was at the same time the roof of a veranda that went along the back of the house, and had a stair at one end to the garden.

Helen was not easily frightened, and had stopped her needle only that she might listen the better. She heard nothing. Of course it was but a fancy! Her hands went on again with their work.—But that was really very like a tap at the window! And now her heart did beat a little faster, if not with fear, then with something very like it, in which perhaps some foreboding was mingled. But she was not a woman to lay down her arms upon the inroad of a vague terror. She quietly rose, and, saying to herself it must be one of the pigeons that haunted the balcony, laid her work on the table, and went to the window. As she drew one of the curtains a little aside to peep, the tap was plainly and hurriedly though softly repeated, and at once she swept it back. There was the dim shadow of a man's head upon the blind, cast there by an old withered moon low in the west! Perhaps it was something in the shape of the shadow that made her pull up the blind so hurriedly, and yet with something of the awe with which we take "the face-cloth from the face." Yes, there was a face!—frightful, not as that of a corpse, but as that of a spectre from whose soul the scars of his mortal end have never passed away. Helen did not scream—her throat seemed to close and her heart to cease. But her eyes continued movelessly fixed on the face even after she knew it was the face of her brother, and the eyes of the face kept staring back into hers through the glass with such a look of concentrated eagerness that they seemed no more organs of vision, but caves of hunger, nor was there a movement of the lips towards speech. The two gazed at each other for a moment of rigid silence.

The glass that separated them might have been the veil that divides those who call themselves the living from those whom they call the dead.

It was but a moment by the clock, though to the after-consciousness it seemed space immeasurable. She came to herself, and slowly, noiselessly, though with tremulous hand, undid the sash, and opened the window. Nothing divided them now, yet he stood as before, staring into her face. Presently his lips began to move, but no words came from them.

In Helen, horror had already roused the instinct of secrecy. She put out her two hands, took his face between them, and said in a hurried whisper, calling him by the pet name she had given him when a child,

"Come in, Poldie, and tell me all about it."

Her voice seemed to wake him. Slowly, with the movements of one half paralyzed, he shoved and dragged himself over the windowsill, dropped himself on the floor inside, and lay there, looking up in her face like a hunted animal, that hoped he had found a refuge, but doubted. Seeing him so exhausted, she turned from him to go and get some brandy, but a low cry of agony drew her back. His head was raised from the floor and his hands were stretched out, while his face entreated her, as plainly as if he had spoken, not to leave him. She knelt and would have kissed him, but he turned his face from her with an expression which seemed of disgust.

"Poldie," she said, "I MUST go and get you something. Don't be afraid. They are all sound asleep."

The grasp with which he had clutched her dress relaxed, and his hand fell by his side. She rose at once and went, creeping through the slumberous house, light and noiseless as a shadow, but with a heart that seemed not her own lying hard in her bosom. As she went she had to struggle both to rouse and to compose herself, for she could not think. An age seemed to have passed since she heard the clock strike twelve. One thing was clear—her brother had been doing something wrong, and dreading discovery, had fled to her. The moment this conviction made itself plain to her, she drew herself up with the great deep breath of a vow, as strong as it was silent and undefined, that he should not have come to her in vain. Silent-footed as a beast of prey, silent-handed as a thief, lithe in her movements, her eye flashing with the new-kindled instinct of motherhood to the orphan of her father, it was as if her soul had been suddenly raised to a white heat, which rendered her body elastic and responsive.

CHAPTER XXII.

LEOPOLD.

She re-entered her room with the gait of a new-born goddess treading the air. Her brother was yet prostrate where she had left him. He raised himself on his elbow, seized with trembling hand the glass she offered him, swallowed the brandy at a gulp, and sank again on the floor. The next instant he sprang to his feet, cast a terrified look at the window, bounded to the door and locked it, then ran to his sister, threw his arms about her, and clung to her like a trembling child. But ever his eyes kept turning to the window.

Though now twenty years of age, and at his full height, he was hardly so tall as Helen. Swarthy of complexion, his hair dark as the night, his eyes large and lustrous, with what Milton calls "quel sereno fulgor d' amabil nero," his frame nervous and slender, he looked compact and small beside her.

She did her utmost to quiet him, unconsciously using the same words and tones with which she had soothed his passions when he was a child. All at once he raised his head and drew himself back from her arms with a look of horror, then put his hand over his eyes, as if her face had been a mirror and he had seen himself in it.

"What is that on your wristband, Leopold?" she asked. "Have you hurt yourself?"

The youth cast an indescribable look on his hand, but it was not that which turned Helen so deadly sick: with her question had come to her the ghastly suspicion that the blood she saw was not his, and she felt guilty of an unpardonable, wicked wrong against him. But she would never, never believe it! A sister suspect her only brother of such a crime! Yet her arms dropped and let him go. She stepped back a pace, and of themselves, as it were, her eyes went wandering and questioning all over him, and saw that his clothes were torn and soiled—stained—who could tell with what?

He stood for a moment still and submissive to their search, with face downcast. Then, suddenly flashing his eyes on her, he said, in a voice that seemed to force its way through earth that choked it back,

"Helen, I am a murderer, and they are after me. They will be here before daylight."

He dropped on his knees, and clasped hers.

"O sister! sister! save me, save me!" he cried in a voice of agony.

Helen stood without response, for to stand took all her strength. How long she fought that horrible sickness, knowing that, if she moved an inch, turned from it a moment, yielded a hair's-breadth, it would throw her senseless on the floor, and the noise of her fall would rouse the house, she never could even conjecture. All was dark before her, as if her gaze had been on the underside of her coffin-lid, and her brain sank and swayed and swung in the coils of the white snake that was sucking at her heart. At length the darkness thinned; it grew a gray mist; the face of her boy-brother glimmered up through it, like that of Dives in hell-fire to his guardian-angel as he hung lax-winged and faint in the ascending smoke. The mist thinned, and at length she caught a glimmer of his pleading, despairing, self-horrified eyes: all the mother in her nature rushed to the aid of her struggling will; her heart gave a great heave; the blood ascended to her white brain, and flushed it with rosy life; her body was once more reconciled and obedient; her hand went forth, took his head between them, and pressed it against her.

"Poldie, dear," she said, "be calm and reasonable, and I will do all I can for you. Here, take this.—And now, answer me one question"

"You won't give me up, Helen?"

"No. I will not."

"Swear it, Helen."

"Ah, my poor Poldie! is it come to this between you and me?"

"Swear it, Helen."

"So help me God, I will not!" returned Helen, looking up.

Leopold rose, and again stood quietly before her, but again with downbent head, like a prisoner about to receive sentence.

"Do you mean what you said a moment since—that the police are in search of you?" asked Helen, with forced calmness.

"They must be. They must have been after me for days—I don't know how many. They will be here soon. I can't think how I have escaped them so long. Hark! Isn't that a noise at the street-door?—No, no.—There's a shadow on the curtains!—No! it's my eyes; they've cheated me a thousand times. Helen! I did not try to hide her; they must have found her long ago."

"My God!" cried Helen; but checked the scream that sought to follow the cry.

"There was an old shaft near," he went on, hurriedly. "If I had thrown her down that, they would never have found her, for there must be choke-damp at the bottom of it enough to kill a thousand of them. But I could not bear the thought of sending the lovely thing down there—even to save my life."

He was growing wild again; but the horror had again laid hold upon Helen, and she stood speechless, staring at him.

"Hide me—hide me, Helen!" he pleaded. "Perhaps you think I am mad. Would to God I were! Sometimes I think I must be. But this I tell you is no madman's fancy. If you take it for that, you will bring me to the gallows. So, if you will see me hanged,——"

He sat down and folded his arms.

"Hush! Poldie, hush!" cried Helen, in an agonized whisper. "I am only thinking what I can best do. I cannot hide you here, for if my aunt knew, she would betray you by her terrors; and if she did not know, and those men came, she would help them to search every corner of the house. Otherwise there might be a chance."

Again she was silent for a few moments; then, seeming suddenly to have made up her mind, went softly to the door.

"Don't leave me!" cried Leopold.

"Hush! I must. I know now what to do. Be quiet here until I come back."

Slowly, cautiously, she unlocked it, and left the room. In three or four minutes she returned, carrying a loaf of bread and a bottle of wine. To her dismay Leopold had vanished. Presently he came creeping out from under the bed, looking so abject that Helen could not help a pang of shame. But the next moment the love of the sister, the tender compassion of the woman, returned in full tide, and swallowed up the unsightly thing. The more abject he was, the more was he to be pitied and ministered to.

"Here, Poldie," she said, "you carry the bread, and I will take the wine. You must eat something, or you will be ill."

As she spoke she locked the door again. Then she put a dark shawl over her head, and fastened it under her chin. Her white face shone out from it like the moon from a dark cloud.

"Follow me, Poldie," she said, and putting out the candles, went to the window.

He obeyed without question, carrying the loaf she had put into his hands. The window-sash rested on a little door; she opened it, and stepped on the balcony. As soon as her brother had followed her, she closed it again, drew down the sash, and led the way to the garden, and so, by the door in the sunk fence, out upon the meadows.

CHAPTER XXIII.

THE REFUGE.

The night was very dusky, but Helen knew perfectly the way she was going. A strange excitement possessed her, and lifted her above all personal fear. The instant she found herself in the open air, her faculties seemed to come preternaturally awake, and her judgment to grow quite cool. She congratulated herself that there had been no rain, and the ground would not betray their steps. There was enough of light in the sky to see the trees against it, and partly by their outlines she guided herself to the door in the park-paling, whence she went as straight as she could for the deserted house. Remembering well her brother's old dislike to the place, she said nothing of their destination; but, when he suddenly stopped, she knew that it had dawned upon him. For one moment he hung back, but a stronger and more definite fear lay behind, and he went on.

Emerging from the trees on the edge of the hollow, they looked down, but it was too dark to see the mass of the house, or the slightest gleam from the surface of the lake. All was silent as a deserted churchyard, and they went down the slope as if it had been the descent to Hades. Arrived at the wall of the garden, they followed its buttressed length until they came to a tall narrow gate of wrought iron, almost consumed with rust, and standing half open. By this they passed into the desolate garden, whose misery in the daytime was like that of a ruined soul, but now hidden in the night's black mantle. Through the straggling bushes with their arms they forced and with their feet they felt their way to the front door of the house, the steps to which, from the effects of various floods, were all out of the level in different directions. The door was unlocked as usual, needing only a strong push to open it, and they entered. How awfully still it seemed!—much stiller than the open air, though that had seemed noiseless. There was not a rat or a black beetle in the place. They groped their way through the hall, and up the wide staircase, which gave not one crack in answer to their needlessly careful footsteps: not a soul was within a mile of them. Helen had taken Leopold by the hand, and she now led him straight to the closet whence the hidden room opened. He made no resistance, for the covering wings of the darkness had protection in them. How desolate must the soul be that welcomes such protection! But when, knowing that thence no ray could reach the outside, she struck a light, and the spot where he had so often shuddered was laid bare to his soul, he gave a cry and turned and would have rushed away. Helen caught him, he yielded, and allowed her to lead him into the room. There she lighted a candle, and as it came gradually alive, it shed a pale yellow light around, and revealed a bare chamber, with a bedstead and the remains of a moth-eaten mattress in a corner. Leopold threw himself upon it, uttering a sound that more resembled a choked scream than a groan. Helen sat down beside him, took his head on her lap, and sought to soothe him with such tender loving words as had never before found birth in her heart, not to say crossed her lips. She took from her pocket a dainty morsel, and tried to make him eat, but in vain. Then she poured him out a cupful of wine. He drank it eagerly, and asked for more, which she would not give him. But instead of comforting him, it seemed only to rouse him to fresh horror. He clung to his sister as a child clings to the nurse who has just been telling him an evil tale, and ever his face would keep turning from her to the door with a look of frightful anticipation. She consoled him with all her ingenuity, assured him that for the present he was perfectly safe, and, thinking it would encourage a sense of concealment, reminded him of the trap in the floor of the closet and the little chamber underneath. But at that he started up with glaring eyes.

"Helen! I remember now," he cried. "I knew it at the time! Don't you know I never could endure the place? I foresaw, as plainly as I see you now, that one day I should be crouching here for safety with a hideous crime on my conscience. I told you so, Helen, at the time. Oh! how could you bring me here?"

He threw himself down again, and hid his face on her lap.

With a fresh inroad of dismay Helen thought he must be going mad, for this was the merest trick of his imagination. Certainly he had always dreaded the place, but never a word of that sort had he said to her. Yet there was a shadow of possible comfort in the thought—for, what if the whole thing should prove an hallucination! But whether real or not, she must have his story.

"Come, dearest Poldie, darling brother!" she said, "you have not yet told me what it is. What is the terrible thing you have done? I daresay it's nothing so very bad after all!"

"There's the light coming!" he said, in a dull hollow voice, "—The morning! always the morning coming again!"

"No, no, dear Poldie!" she returned. "There is no window here—at least it only looks on the back stair, high above heads; and the morning is a long way off."

"How far?" he asked, staring in her eyes—"twenty years? That was just when I was born! Oh that I could enter a second time into my mother's womb, and never be born! Why are we sent into this cursed world? I would God had never made it. What was the good? Couldn't he have let well alone?"

He was silent. She must get him to sleep.

It was as if a second soul had been given her to supplement the first, and enable her to meet what would otherwise have been the exorbitant demands now made upon her. With an effort of the will such as she could never before have even imagined, she controlled the anguish of her own spirit, and, softly stroking the head of the poor lad, which had again sought her lap, compelled herself to sing him for lullaby a song of which in his childhood he had been very fond, and with which, in all the importance of imagined motherhood, she had often sung him to sleep. And the old influence was potent yet. In a few minutes the fingers which clutched her hand relaxed, and she knew by his breathing that he slept. She sat still as a stone, not daring to move, hardly daring breathe enough to keep her alive, lest she should rouse him from his few blessed moments of self-nothingness, during which the tide of the all-infolding ocean of peace was free to flow into the fire-torn cave of his bosom. She sat motionless thus, until it seemed as if for very weariness she must drop in a heap on the floor, but that the aches and pains which went through her in all directions held her body together like ties and rivets. She had never before known what weariness was, and now she knew it for all her life. But like an irritant, her worn body clung about her soul and dulled it to its own grief, thus helping it to a pitiful kind of repose. How long she sat thus she could not tell—she had no means of knowing, but it seemed hours on hours, and yet, though the nights were now short, the darkness had not begun to thin. But when she thought how little access the light had to that room, she began to grow uneasy lest she should be missed from her own, or seen on her way back to it. At length some involuntary movement woke him. He started to his feet with a look of wild gladness. But there was scarcely time to recognise it before it vanished.

"My God, it is true then!" he shrieked. "O Helen, I dreamed that I was innocent—that I had but dreamed I had done it. Tell me that I'm dreaming now. Tell me! tell me!—Tell me that I am no murderer!"

As he spoke, he seized her shoulder with a fierce grasp, and shook her as if trying to wake her from the silence of a lethargy.

"I hope you are innocent, my darling. But in any case I will do all I can to protect you," said Helen. "Only I shall never be able unless you control yourself sufficiently to let me go home."

"No, Helen!" he cried; "you must not leave me. If you do, I shall go mad. SHE will come instead."

Helen shuddered inwardly, but kept her outward composure.

"If I stay with you, just think, dearest, what will happen," she said. "I shall be missed, and all the country will be raised to look for me. They will think I have been—"—She checked herself.

"And so you might be—so might anyone," he cried, "so long as I am loose—like the Rajah's man-eating horse. O God! It has come to this!" And he hid his face in his hands.

"And then you see, my Poldie," Helen went on as calmly as she could, "they would come here and find us; and I don't know what might come next."

"Yes, yes, Helen! Go, go directly. Leave me this instant," he said, hurriedly, and took her by the shoulders, as if he would push her from the room, but went on talking. "It must be, I know; but when the light comes I shall go mad. Would to God I might, for the day is worse than the darkness; then I see my own black against the light. Now go, Helen. But you WILL come back to me as soon as ever you can? How shall I know when to begin to look for you? What o'clock is it? My watch has never been—since—. Ugh! the light will be here soon. Helen, I know now what hell is.—Ah! Yes."—As he spoke he had been feeling in one of his pockets.—"I will not be taken alive.—Can you whistle, Helen?"

"Yes, Poldie," answered Helen, trembling. "Don't you remember teaching me?"

"Yes, yes.—Then, when you come near the house, whistle, and go on whistling, for if I hear a step without any whistling, I shall kill myself."

"What have you got there?" she asked in renewed terror, noticing that he kept his hand in the breast pocket of his coat.

"Only the knife," he answered calmly.

"Give it to me," she said, calmly too.

He laughed, and the laugh was more terrible than any cry.

"No; I'm not so green as that," he said. "My knife is my only friend! Who is to take care of me when you are away? Ha! ha!"

She saw that the comfort of the knife must not be denied him. Nor did she fear any visit that might drive him to its use—except indeed the police WERE to come upon him—and then—what better could he do? she thought.

"Well, well, I will not plague you," she said. "Lie down and I will cover you with my shawl, and you can fancy it my arms round you. I will come to you as soon as ever I can."

He obeyed. She spread her shawl over him and kissed him.

"Thank you, Helen," he said quietly.

"Pray to God to deliver you, dear," she said.

"He can do that only by killing me," he returned. "I will pray for that. But do you go, Helen. I will try to bear my misery for your sake."

He followed her from the room with eyes out of which looked the very demon of silent despair.

I will not further attempt to set forth his feelings. The incredible, the impossible, had become a fact-AND HE WAS THE MAN. He who knows the relief of waking from a dream of crime to the jubilation of recovered innocence, to the sunlight that blots out the thing as untrue, may by help of that conceive the misery of a delicate nature suddenly filled with the clear assurance of horrible guilt. Such a misery no waking but one that annihilated the past could ever console. Yes, there is yet an awaking—if a man might but attain unto it—an awaking into a region whose very fields are full of the harmony sovereign to console, not merely for having suffered—that needs little consoling, but for having inflicted the deepest wrong.

The moment Helen was out of sight, Leopold drew a small silver box from an inner pocket, eyed it with the eager look of a hungry animal, took from it a portion of a certain something, put it in his mouth, closed his eyes, and lay still.

CHAPTER XXIV.

HELEN WITH A SECRET.

When Helen came out into the corridor, she saw that the day was breaking. A dim, dreary light filled the dismal house, but the candle had prevented her from perceiving the little of it that could enter that room withdrawn. A pang of fear shot to her soul, and like a belated spectre or a roused somnambulist she fled across the park. It was all so like a horrible dream, from which she must wake in bed! yet she knew there was no such hope for her. Her darling lay in that frightful house, and if anyone should see her, it might be death to him. But yet it was very early, and two hours would pass before any of the workmen would be on their way to the new house. Yet, like a murderer shaken out of the earth by the light, she fled. When she was safe in her own room, ere she could get into bed, she once more turned deadly sick, and next knew by the agonies of coming to herself that she had fainted.

A troubled, weary, EXCITED sleep followed. She woke with many a start, as if she had sinned in sleeping, and instantly for very weariness, dozed off again. How kind is weariness sometimes! It is like the Father's hand laid a little heavy on the heart to make it still. But her dreams were full of torture, and even when she had no definite dream, she was haunted by the vague presence of blood. It was considerably past her usual time for rising when at length she heard her maid in the room. She got up wearily, but beyond the heaviest of hearts and a general sense of misery, nothing ailed her. Nor even did her head ache.

But she had lived an age since she woke last; and the wonder was, not that she felt so different, but that she should be aware of being the same person as before notwithstanding all that had passed. Her business now was to keep herself from thinking until breakfast should be over. She must hold the "ebony box" of last night close shut even from her own eyes, lest the demons of which it was full should rush out and darken the world about her. She hurried to her bath for strength: the friendly water would rouse her to the present, make the past recede like a dream, and give her courage to face the future. Her very body seemed defiled by the knowledge that was within it. Alas! how must poor Leopold feel, then! But she must not think.

All the time she was dressing, her thoughts kept hovering round the awful thing like moths around a foul flame, from which she could not drive them away. Ever and again she said to herself that she must not, yet ever and again she found herself peeping through the chinks of the thought-chamber at the terrible thing inside—the form of which she could not see—saw only the colour—red,—red mingled with ghastly whiteness. In all the world, her best-loved, her brother, the child of her grandfather, was the only one who knew how that thing came there.

But while Helen's being was in such tumult that she could never more be the cool, indifferent, self-contented person she had hitherto been, her old habits and forms of existence were now of endless help to the retaining of her composure and the covering of her secret. A dim gleam of gladness woke in her at the sight of the unfinished cap, than which she could not have a better excuse for her lateness, and when she showed it to her aunt with the wish of many happy returns of the day, no second glance from Mrs. Ramshorn added to her uneasiness.

But oh, how terribly the time crept in its going! for she dared not approach the deserted house while the daylight kept watching it like a dog; and what if Leopold should have destroyed himself in the madness of his despair before she could go to him! She had not a friend to help her. George Bascombe?— she shuddered at the thought of him. With his grand ideas of duty, he would be for giving up Leopold that very moment! Naturally the clergyman was the one to go to—and Mr. Wingfold had himself done wrong. But he had confessed it! No—he was a poor creature, and would not hold his tongue! She shook at every knock at the door, every ring at the bell, lest it should be the police. To be sure, he had been comparatively little there, and naturally they would seek him first at Goldswyre—but where next? At Glaston, of course. Every time a servant entered the room she turned away, lest her ears should make her countenance a traitor. The police might be watching the house, and might follow her when she went to him! With her opera-glass, she examined the meadow, then ran to the bottom of the garden, and lying down, peered over the sunk fence. But not a human being was in sight. Next she put on her bonnet, with the pretence of shopping, to see if there were any suspicious-looking persons in the street. But she did not meet a single person unknown to her between her aunt's door and Mr. Drew the linendraper's. There she bought a pair of gloves, and walked quietly back, passing the house, and going on to the Abbey, without meeting one person at whom she had to look twice.

All the time her consciousness was like a single intense point of light in the middle of a darkness it could do nothing to illuminate. She knew nothing but that her brother lay in that horrible empty house, and that, if his words were not the ravings of a maniac, the law, whether it yet suspected him or not, was certainly after him, and if it had not yet struck upon his trail, was every moment on the point of finding it, and must sooner or later come up with him. She MUST save him—all that was left of him to save! But poor Helen knew very little about saving.

One thing more she became suddenly aware of as she re-entered the house—the possession of a power of dissimulation, of hiding herself, hitherto strange to her, for hitherto she had had nothing, hardly even a passing dislike to conceal. The consciousness brought only exultation with it, for her nature was not yet delicate enough to feel the jar of the thought that neither words nor looks must any more be an index to what lay within her.

CHAPTER XXV.

A DAYLIGHT VISIT.

But she could not rest. When would the weary day be over, and the longed-for rather than welcome night appear? Again she went into the garden, and down to the end of it, and looked out over the meadow. Not a creature was in sight, except a red and white cow, a child gathering buttercups, and a few rooks crossing from one field to another. It was a glorious day; the sun seemed the very centre of conscious peace. And now first, strange to say, Helen began to know the bliss of bare existence under a divine sky, in the midst of a divine air, the two making a divine summer, which throbbed with the presence of the creative spirit—but as something apart from her now, something she had had, but had lost, which could never more be hers. How could she ever be glad again, with such a frightful fact in her soul! Away there beyond those trees lay her unhappy brother, in the lonely house, now haunted indeed. Perhaps he lay there dead! The horrors of the morning, or his own hand, might have slain him. She must go to him. She would defy the very sun, and go in the face of the universe. Was he not her brother?—Was there no help anywhere? no mantle for this sense of soul-nakedness that had made her feel as if her awful secret might be read a mile away, lying crimson and livid in the bottom of her heart. She dared hardly think of it, lest the very act should betray the thing of darkness to the world of light around her. Nothing but the atmosphere of another innocent soul could shield hers, and she had no friend. What did people do when their brothers did awful deeds? She had heard of praying to God—had indeed herself told her brother to pray, but it was all folly—worse, priestcraft. As if such things AND a God could exist together! Yet, even with the thought of denial in her mind, she looked up, and gazed earnestly into the wide innocent mighty space, as if by searching she might find some one. Perhaps she OUGHT to pray. She could see no likelihood of a God, and yet something pushed her towards prayer. What if all this had come upon her and Poldie because she never prayed! If there were such horrible things in the world, although she had never dreamed of them—if they could come so near her, into her very soul, making her feel like a murderess, might there not be a God also, though she knew nothing of his whereabouts or how to reach him and gain a hearing? Certainly if things went with such hellish possibilities at the heart of them, and there was no hand at all to restrain or guide or restore, the world was a good deal worse place than either the Methodists or the Positivists made it out to be. In the form of feelings, not of words, hardly even of thoughts, things like these passed through her mind as she stood on the top of the sunk fence and gazed across the flat of sunny green before her. She could almost have slain herself to be rid of her knowledge and the awful consciousness that was its result.

SHE would have found no difficulty in that line of Macbeth:—"To know my deed, 'twere best not know myself."—But all this time there was her brother! She MUST go to him. "God hide me," she cried within her. "But how can he hide me," she thought, "when I am hiding a murderer?" "O God," she cried again, and this time in an audible murmur, "I am his sister, thou knowest!" Then she turned, walked back to the house, and sought her aunt.

"I have got a little headache," she said quite coolly, "and I want a long walk. Don't wait luncheon for me. It is such a glorious day! I shall go by the Millpool road, and across the park. Good-bye till tea, or perhaps dinner-time even."

"Hadn't you better have a ride and be back to luncheon? I shan't want Jones to-day," said her aunt mournfully, who, although she had almost given up birthdays, thought her niece need not quite desert her on the disagreeable occasion.

"I'm not in tne humour for riding, aunt. Nothing will do me good but a walk. I shall put some luncheon in my bag."

She went quietly out by the front door, walked slowly, softly, statelily along the street and out of the town, and entered the park by the lodge-gate. She saw Rachel at her work in the kitchen as she passed, and heard her singing in a low and weak but very sweet voice, which went to her heart like a sting, making the tall, handsome, rich lady envy the poor distorted atom who, through all the fogs of her winter, had yet something in her that sought such utterance. But, indeed, if all her misery had been swept away like a dream, Helen might yet have envied the dwarf ten times more than she did now, had she but known how they stood compared with each other. For the being of Helen to that of Rachel was as a single, untwined primary cell to a finished brain; as the peeping of a chicken to the song of a lark—I had almost said, to a sonata of Beethoven.

"Good day, Rachel," she said, calling as she passed, in a kindly, even then rather condescending voice, through the open door, where a pail of water, just set down, stood rocking the sun on its heaving surface, and flashing it out again into the ocean of the light. It seemed to poor Helen a squalid abode, but it was a home-like palace, and fairly furnished, in comparison with the suburban villa and shop-upholstery which typified the house of her spirit— now haunted by a terrible secret walking through its rooms, and laying a bloody hand upon all their whitenesses.

There was no sound all the way as she went but the noise of the birds, and an occasional clank from the new building far away. At last, with beating heart and scared soul, she was within the high garden-wall, making her way through the rank growth of weeds and bushes to the dismal house. She entered trembling, and the air felt as if death had been before her. Hardly would her limbs carry her, but with slow step she reached the hidden room. He lay as she had left him. Was he asleep, or dead? She crept near and laid her hand on his forehead. He started to his feet in an agony of fright. She soothed and reassured him as best she was able. When the paroxysm relaxed—

"You didn't whistle," he said.

"No; I forgot," answered Helen, shocked at her own carelessness. "But if I had, you would not have heard me: you were fast asleep."

"A good thing I was! And yet no! I wish I had heard you, for then by this time I should have been beyond their reach."

Impulsively he showed her the short dangerous looking weapon he carried. Helen stretched out her hand to take it, but he hurriedly replaced it in his pocket.

"I will find some water for you to wash with," said Helen. "There used to be a well in the garden, I remember. I have brought you a shirt."

With some difficulty she found the well, all but lost in matted weeds under an ivy-tod, and in the saucer of a flower-pot she carried him some water, and put the garment with the horrible spot in her bag, to take it away and destroy it. Then she made him eat and drink. He did whatever she told him, with a dull, yet doglike obedience. His condition was much changed; he had a stupefied look, and seemed only half awake to his terrible situation. Yet he answered what questions she put to him even too readily—with an indifferent matter-of-factness, indeed, more dreadful than any most passionate outburst. But at the root of the apparent apathy lay despair and remorse,—weary, like gorged and sleeping tigers far back in their dens. Only the dull torpedo of misery was awake, lying motionless on the bottom of the deepest pool of his spirit.

The mood was favourable to the drawing of his story from him, but there are more particulars in the narrative I am now going to give than Helen at that time learned.

CHAPTER XXVI.

LEOPOLD'S STORY.

While yet a mere boy, scarcely more than sixteen, Leopold had made acquaintance with the family of a certain manufacturer, who, having retired from business with a rapidly-gained fortune, had some years before purchased an estate a few miles from Goldswyre, his uncle's place. Their settling in the neighbourhood was not welcome to the old-fashioned, long-rooted family of the Lingards; but although they had not called upon them, they could not help meeting them occasionally. Leopold's association with them commenced just after he had left Eton, between which time and his going up to Cambridge he spent a year in reading with his cousins' tutor. It was at a ball he first saw Emmeline, the eldest of the family. She had but lately returned from a school at which from the first she had had for her bedfellow a black ewe. It was not a place where any blackness under that of pitch was likely to attract notice, being one of those very ordinary and very common schools where everything is done that is done, first for manners, then for accomplishments, and lastly for information, leaving all the higher faculties and endowments of the human being as entirely unconsidered as if they had no existence. Taste, feeling, judgment, imagination, conscience, are in such places left to look after themselves, and the considerations presented to them, and duties required of them as religious, are only fitted to lower still farther such moral standard as they may possess. Schools of this kind send out, as their quota of the supply of mothers for the ages to come, young women who will consult a book of etiquette as to what is ladylike; who always think what is the mode, never what is beautiful; who read romances in which the wickedness is equalled only by the shallowness; who write questions to weekly papers concerning points of behaviour, and place their whole, or chief delight in making themselves attractive to men. Some such girls look lady-like and interesting, and many of them are skilled in the arts that meet their fullest development in a nature whose sense of existence is rounded by its own reflection in the mirror of self-consciousness falsified by vanity. Once understood, they are for a sadness or a loathing, after the nature that understands them; till then, they are to the beholder such as they desire to appear, while under the fair outside lies a nature whose vulgarity, if the most thorough of changes do not in the meantime supervene, will manifest itself hideously on the approach of middle age, that is, by the time when habituation shall have destroyed the restraints of diffidence. Receiving ever fresh and best assurance of their own consequence in the attention and admiration of men, such girls are seldom capable of any real attachment, and the marvel is that so few of them comparatively disgrace themselves after marriage.

Whether it was the swarthy side of his nature, early ripened under the hot Indian sun, that found itself irresistibly drawn to the widening of its humanity in the flaxen fairness of Emmeline, or the Saxon element in him seeking back to its family—it might indeed have been both, our nature admitting of such marvellous complexity in its unity,—he fell in love with her, if not in the noblest yet in a very genuine, though at the same time very passionate way; and as she had, to use a Scots proverb, a crop for all corn, his attentions were acceptable to her. Had she been true-hearted enough to know anything of that love whose name was for ever suffering profanation upon her lips, she would, being at least a year and a half older than he, have been too much of a woman to encourage his approaches—would have felt he was a boy and must not be allowed to fancy himself a man. But to be just, he did look to English eyes older than he was. And then he was very handsome, distinguished-looking, of a good family, which could in no sense be said of her,—and with high connections—at the same time a natural contrast to herself, and personally attractive to her. The first moment she saw his great black eyes blaze, she accepted the homage, laid it on the altar of her self-worship, and ever after sought to see them lighted up afresh in worship of her only divinity. To be feelingly aware of her power over him, to play upon him as on an instrument, to make his cheek pale or glow, his eyes flash or fill, as she pleased, was a game almost too delightful.

One of the most potent means for producing the humano-atmospheric play in which her soul thus rejoiced, and one whose operation was to none better known than to Emmeline, was jealousy, and for its generation she had all possible facilities—for there could not be a woman in regard of whom jealousy was more justifiable on any ground except that of being worth it. So far as it will reach, however, it must be remembered, in mitigation of judgment, that she had no gauge in herself equal to the representation of a tithe of the misery whose signs served to lift her to the very Paradise of falsehood: she knew not what she did, and possibly knowledge might have found in her some pity and abstinence. But when a woman, in her own nature cold, takes delight in rousing passion, she will, selfishly confident in her own safety, go to strange lengths in kindling and fanning the flame which is the death of the other.

It is far from my intention to follow the disagreeable topic across the pathless swamp through which an elaboration of its phases would necessarily drag me. Of morbid anatomy, save for the setting forth of cure, I am not fond, and here there is nothing to be said of cure. What concerns me as a narrator is, that Emmeline consoled and irritated and re-consoled Leopold, until she had him her very slave, and the more her slave that by that time he knew something of her character. The knowledge took from him what little repose she had left him; he did no more good at school, and went to Cambridge with the conviction that the woman to whom he had given his soul, would be doing things in his absence the sight of which would drive him mad. Yet somehow he continued to live, reassured now and then by the loving letters she wrote to him, and relieving his own heart while he fostered her falsehood by the passionate replies he made to them.

From a sad accident of his childhood, he had become acquainted with something of the influences of a certain baneful drug, to the use of which one of his attendants was addicted, and now at college, partly from curiosity, partly from a desire to undergo its effects, but chiefly in order to escape from ever-gnawing and passionate thought, he began to make EXPERIMENTS in its use. Experiment called for repetition—in order to verification, said the fiend,—and repetition led first to a longing after its effects, and next to a mad appetite for the thing itself; so that, by the time of which my narrative treats, he was on the verge of absolute slavery to its use, and in imminent peril of having to pass the rest of his life in alternations of ecstasy and agony, divided by dull spaces of misery, the ecstasies growing rarer and rarer, and the agonies more and more frequent, intense, and lasting; until at length the dethroned Apollo found himself chained to a pillar of his own ruined temple, which the sirocco was fast filling with desert sand.

CHAPTER XXVII.

LEOPOLD'S STORY CONCLUDED.

He knew from her letters that they were going to give a ball, at which as many as pleased should be welcome in fancy dresses, and masked if they chose. The night before it he had a dream, under the influence of his familiar no doubt, which made him so miserable and jealous that he longed to see her as a wounded man longs for water, and the thought arose of going down to the ball, not exactly in disguise, for he had no mind to act a part, but masked so that he should not be recognised as uninvited, and should have an opportunity of watching Emmeline, concerning whose engagement with a young cavalry officer there had lately been reports, which, however, before his dream, had caused him less uneasiness than many such preceding. The same moment the thought was a resolve.

I must mention that no one whatever knew the degree of his intimacy with Emmeline, or that he had any ground for considering her engaged to him. Secrecy added much to the zest of Emmeline's pleasures. Everyone knew that he was a devoted admirer—but therein to be classed with a host.

For concealment, he contented himself with a large travelling-cloak, a tall felt hat, and a black silk mask.

He entered the grounds with an arrival of guests, and knowing the place perfectly, contrived to see something of her behaviour, while he watched for an opportunity of speaking to her alone,—a quest of unlikely success. Hour after hour he watched, and all the time never spoke or was spoken to.

Those who are acquainted with the mode of operation of the drug to which I have referred, are aware that a man may be fully under its influences without betraying to the ordinary observer that he is in a condition differing from that of other men. But, in the living dream wherein he walks, his feeling of time and of space is so enlarged, or perhaps, I rather think, so subdivided to the consciousness, that everything about him seems infinite both in duration and extent; the action of a second has in it a multitudinous gradation of progress, and a line of space is marked out into millionths, of every one of which the consciousness takes note. At the same time his senses are open to every impression from things around him, only they appear to him in a strangely exalted metamorphosis, the reflex of his own mental exaltation either in bliss or torture, while the fancies of a man mingle with the facts thus introduced and modify and are in turn modified by them; whereby out of the chaos arises the mountain of an Earthly Paradise, whose roots are in the depths of hell; and whether the man be with the divine air and the clear rivers and the thousand-hued flowers on the top, or down in the ice-lake with the tears frozen to hard lumps in the hollows of his eyes so that he can no more have even the poor consolation of weeping, is but the turning of a hair, so far at least as his will has to do with it. The least intrusion of anything painful, of any jar that cannot be wrought into the general harmony of the vision, will suddenly alter its character, and from the seventh heaven of speechless bliss the man may fall plumb down into gulfs of horrible and torturing, it may be loathsome imaginings.

Now Leopold had taken a dose of the drug on his journey, and it was later than usual, probably because of the motion, ere it began to take effect. He had indeed ceased to look for any result from it, when all at once, as he stood amongst the laburnums and lilacs of a rather late spring, something seemed to burst in his brain, and that moment he was Endymion waiting for Diana in her interlunar grove, while the music of the spheres made the blossoms of a stately yet flowering forest, tremble all with conscious delight.

Emboldened by his new condition, he drew nigh the house. They were then passing from the ball to the supper-room, and he found the tumult so distasteful to his mood of still ecstasy that he would not have entered had he not remembered that he had in his pocket a note ready if needful to slip into her hand, containing only the words, "Meet me for one long minute at the circle,"—a spot well known to both: he threw his cloak Spanish fashion over his left shoulder, slouched his hat, and entering stood in a shadowy spot she must pass in going to or from the supper-room. There he waited, with the note hid in his hand—a long time, yet not a weary one, such visions of loveliness passed before his entranced gaze. At length SHE also passed— lovely as the Diana whose dress she had copied—not quite so perfectly as she had abjured her manners. She leaned trustingly on the arm of some one, but Leopold never even looked at him. He slid the note into her hand, which hung ungloved as inviting confidences. With an instinct quickened and sharpened tenfold by much practice, her fingers instantly closed upon it, but, not a muscle belonging to any other part of her betrayed the intrusion of a foreign body: I do not believe her heart gave one beat the more to the next minute. She passed graceful on, her swan's-neck shining; and Leopold hastened out to one of the windows of the ball-room, there to feast his eyes upon her loveliness. But when he caught sight of her whirling in the waltz with the officer of dragoons whose name he had heard coupled with hers, and saw her flash on him the light and power of eyes which were to him the windows of all the heaven he knew, as they swam together in the joy of the rhythm, of the motion, of the music, suddenly the whole frame of the dream wherein he wandered, trembled, shook, fell down into the dreary vaults that underlie all the airy castles that have other foundation than the will of the eternal Builder. With the suddenness of the dark that follows the lightning, the music changed to a dissonant clash of multitudinous cymbals, the resounding clang of brazen doors, and the hundred-toned screams of souls in torture. The same moment, from halls of infinite scope, where the very air was a soft tumult of veiled melodies ever and anon twisted into inextricable knots of harmony—under whose skyey domes he swept upborne by chords of sound throbbing up against great wings mighty as thought yet in their motions as easy and subtle, he found himself lying on the floor of a huge vault, whose black slabs were worn into many hollows by the bare feet of the damned as they went and came between the chambers of their torture opening off upon every side, whence issued all kinds of sickening cries, and mingled with the music to which, with whips of steel, hellish executioners urged the dance whose every motion was an agony. His soul fainted within him, and the vision changed. When he came to himself, he lay on the little plot of grass amongst the lilacs and laburnums where he had asked Emmeline to meet him. Fevered with jealousy and the horrible drug, his mouth was parched like an old purse, and he found himself chewing at the grass to ease its burning and drought. But presently the evil thing resumed its sway and fancies usurped over facts. He thought he was lying in an Indian jungle, close by the cave of a beautiful tigress, which crouched within, waiting the first sting of reviving hunger to devour him. He could hear her breathing as she slept, but he was fascinated, paralyzed, and could not escape, knowing that, even if with mighty effort he succeeded in moving a finger, the motion would suffice to wake her, and she would spring upon him and tear him to pieces. Years upon years passed thus, and he still lay on the grass in the jungle, and still the beautiful tigress slept. But however far apart the knots upon the string of time may lie, they must pass: an angel in white stood over him, his fears vanished, the waving of her wings cooled him, and she was the angel whom he had loved and loved from all eternity, in whom was his ever-and-only rest. She lifted him to his feet, gave him her hand, they walked away, and the tigress was asleep for ever. For miles and miles, as it seemed to his exaltation, they wandered away into the woods, to wander in them for ever, the same violet blue, flashing with roseate stars, for ever looking in through the tree-tops, and the great leafy branches hushing, ever hushing them, as with the voices of child-watching mothers, into peace, whose depth is bliss.

"Have you nothing to say now I am come?" said the angel.

"I have said all. I am at rest," answered the mortal.

"I am going to be married to Captain Hodges," said the angel.

And with the word, the forests of heaven vanished, and the halls of Eblis did not take their place:—a worse hell was there—the cold reality of an earth abjured, and a worthless maiden walking by his side. He stood and turned to her. The shock had mastered the drug. They were only in the little wooded hollow, a hundred yards from the house. The blood throbbed in his head as from the piston of an engine. A horrid sound of dance-music was in his ears. Emmeline, his own, stood in her white dress, looking up in his face, with the words just parted from her lips, "I am going to be married to Captain Hodges." The next moment she threw her arms round his neck, pulled his face to hers, and kissed him, and clung to him.

"Poor Leopold!" she said, and looked in his face with her electric battery at full power; "does it make him miserable, then?—But you know it could not have gone on like this between you and me for ever! It was very dear while it lasted, but it must come to an end."

Was there a glimmer of real pity and sadness in those wondrous eyes? She laughed—was it a laugh of despair or of exultation?—and hid her face on his bosom. And what was it that awoke in Leopold? Had the drug resumed its power over him? Was it rage at her mockery, or infinite compassion for her despair? Would he slay a demon, or ransom a spirit from hateful bonds? Would he save a woman from disgrace and misery to come? or punish her for the vilest falsehood? Who can tell? for Leopold himself never could. Whatever the feeling was, its own violence erased it from his memory, and left him with a knife in his hand, and Emmeline lying motionless at his feet. It was a knife the Scotch highlanders call a skean-dhu, sharp-pointed as a needle, sharp-edged as a razor, and with one blow of it he had cleft her heart, and she never cried or laughed any more in that body whose charms she had degraded to the vile servitude of her vanity. The next thing he remembered was standing on the edge of the shaft of a deserted coalpit, ready to cast himself down. Whence came the change of resolve, he could not tell, but he threw in his cloak and mask, and fled. The one thought in his miserable brain was his sister. Having murdered one woman, he was fleeing to another for refuge. Helen would save him.

How he had found his way to his haven, he had not an idea. Searching the newspapers, Helen heard that a week had elapsed between the "mysterious murder of a young lady in Yorkshire" and the night on which he came to her window.

CHAPTER XXVIII.

SISTERHOOD.

"Well, Poldie, after all I would rather be you than she!" cried Helen indignantly, when she had learned the whole story.

It was far from the wisest thing to say, but she meant it, and clasped her brother to her bosom.

Straightway the poor fellow began to search for all that man could utter in excuse, nay in justification, not of himself, but of the woman he had murdered, appropriating all the blame. But Helen had recognised in Emmeline the selfishness which is the essential murderer, nor did it render her more lenient towards her that the same moment, with a start of horror, she caught a transient glimpse of the same in herself. But the discovery wrought in the other direction, and the tenderness she now lavished upon Leopold left all his hopes far behind. Her brother's sin had broken wide the feebly-flowing springs of her conscience, and she saw that in idleness and ease and drowsiness of soul, she had been forgetting and neglecting even the being she loved best in the universe. In the rushing confluence of love, truth, and indignation, to atone for years of half-love, half-indifference, as the past now appeared to her, she would have spoiled him terribly, heaping on him caresses and assurances that he was far the less guilty and the more injured of the two; but Leopold's strength was exhausted, and he fell back in a faint.

While she was occupied with his restoration many things passed through her mind. Amongst the rest she saw it would be impossible for her to look after him sufficiently where he was, that the difficulty of feeding him even would be great, that very likely he was on the borders of an illness, when he would require constant attention, that the danger of discovery was great—in short, that some better measures must be taken for his protection and the possibility of her ministrations. If she had but a friend to consult! Ever that thought returned. Alas! she had none on whose counsel or discretion either she could depend. When at length he opened his eyes, she told him she must leave him now, but when it was dark she would come again, and stay with him till dawn. Feebly he assented, seeming but half aware of what she said, and again closed his eyes. While he lay thus, she gained possession of his knife. It left its sheath behind it, and she put it naked in her pocket. As she went from the room, feeling like a mother abandoning her child in a wolf-haunted forest, his eyes followed her to the door with a longing, wild, hungry look, and she felt the look following her still through the wood and across the park and into her chamber, while the knife in her pocket felt like a spellbound demon waiting his chance to work them both a mischief. She locked her door and took it out, and as she put it carefully away, fearful lest any attempt to destroy it might lead to its discovery, she caught sight of her brother's name engraved in full upon the silver mounting of the handle. "What if he had left it behind him!" she thought with a shudder.

But a reassuring strength had risen in her mind with Leopold's disclosure. More than once on her way home she caught herself reasoning that the poor boy had not been to blame at all—that he could not help it—that she had deserved nothing less. Her conscience speedily told her that in consenting to such a thought, she herself would be a murderess. Love her brother she must; excuse him she might, for honest excuse is only justice; but to uphold the deed would be to take the part of hell against heaven. Still the murder did not, would not seem so frightful after she had heard the whole tale, and she found it now required far less effort to face her aunt. If she was not the protectress of the innocent, she was of the grievously wronged, and the worst wrong done him was the crime he had been driven to do. She lay down and slept until dinner time, woke refreshed, and sustained her part during the slow meal, neartened by the expectation of seeing her brother again and in circumstance of less anxiety when the friendly darkness had come, and all eyes but theirs were closed. She talked to her aunt and a lady who dined with them as if she had the freest heart in the world; the time passed; the converse waned; the hour arrived; adieus were said; drowsiness came. All the world of Glaston was asleep; the night on her nest was brooding upon the egg of to-morrow; the moon was in darkness; and the wind was blowing upon Helen's hot forehead, as she slid like a thief across the park.

Her mind was in a tumult of mingled feelings, all gathered about the form of her precious brother. One moment she felt herself ministering to the father she had loved so dearly, in protecting his son; the next the thought of her father had vanished, and all was love for the boy whose memories filled the shadow of her childhood; about whom she had dreamed night after night as he crossed the great sea to come to her; who had crept into her arms timidly, and straightway turned into the daintiest merriest playmate; who had charmed her even in his hot-blooded rages, when he rushed at her with whatever was in his hand at the moment. Then she had laughed and dared him; now she shuddered to remember. Again, and this was the feeling that generally prevailed, she was a vessel overflowing with the mere woman-passion of protection: the wronged, abused, maddened, oppressed, hunted human thing was dependent upon her, and her alone, for any help or safety he was ever to find. Sometimes it was the love of a mother for her sick child; sometimes that of a tigress crouching over her wounded cub and licking its hurts. All was coloured with admiration of his beauty and grace, and mingled with boundless pity for their sad overclouding and defeature! Nor was the sense of wrong to herself in wrong to her own flesh and blood wanting. The sum of all was a passionate devotion of her being to the service of her brother.

I suspect that at root the loves of the noble wife, the great-souled mother, and the true sister, are one. Anyhow, they are all but glints on the ruffled waters of humanity of the one changeless enduring Light.

CHAPTER XXIX.

THE SICK-CHAMBER.

She had reached the little iron gate, which hung on one hinge only, and was lifting it from the ground to push it open, when sudden through the stillness came a frightful cry. Had they found him already? Was it a life-and-death struggle going on within? For one moment she stood rooted; the next she flew to the door. When she entered the hall, however, the place was silent as a crypt. Could it have been her imagination? Again, curdling her blood with horror, came the tearing cry, a sort of shout of agony. All in the dark, she flew up the stair, calling him by name, fell twice, rose as if on wings, and flew again until she reached the room. There all was silence and darkness. With trembling hands she found her match-box and struck a light, uttering all the time every soothing word she could think of, while her heart quavered in momentary terror of another shriek. It came just as the match flamed up in her fingers, and an answering shriek from her bosom tore its way through her clenched teeth, and she shuddered like one in an ague. There sat her brother on the edge of the bedstead staring before him with fixed eyes and terror-stricken countenance. He had not heard her enter, and saw neither the light nor her who held it. She made haste to light the candle, with mighty effort talking to him still, in gasps and chokings, but in vain; the ghastly face continued unchanged, and the wide-open eyes remained fixed. She seated herself beside him, and threw her arms around him. It was like embracing a marble statue, so moveless, so irresponsive was he. But presently he gave a kind of shudder, the tension of his frame relaxed, and the soul which had been absorbed in its own visions, came forward to its windows, cast from them a fleeting glance, then dropped the curtains.

"Is it you, Helen?" he said, shuddering, as he closed his eyes and laid his head on her shoulder. His breath was like that of a furnace. His skin seemed on fire. She felt his pulse: it was galloping. He was in a fever—brain-fever, probably, and what was she to do? A thought came to her. Yes, it was the only possible thing. She would take him home. There, with the help of the household, she might have a chance of concealing him—a poor one, certainly! but here, how was she even to keep him to the house in his raving fits?

"Poldie, dear!" she said, "you must come with me. I am going to take you to my own room, where I can nurse you properly, and need not leave you. Do you think you could walk as far?"

"Walk! Yes—quite well: why not?"

"I am afraid you are going to be ill, Poldie; but, however ill you may feel, you must promise me to try and make as little noise as you can, and never cry out if you can help it. When I do like this," she went on, laying her finger on his lips, "you must be silent altogether."

"I will do whatever you tell me, Helen, if you will only promise not to leave me, and, when they come for me, to give me poison."

She promised, and made haste to obliterate every sign that the room had been occupied. She then took his arm and led him out. He was very quiet—too quiet and submissive, she thought—seemed sleepy, revived a little when they reached the open air, presently grew terrified, and kept starting and looking about him as they crossed the park, but never spoke a word. By the door in the sunk fence they reached the garden, and were soon in Helen's chamber, where she left him to get into bed while she went to acquaint her aunt of his presence in the house. Hard and unreasonable, like most human beings, where her prejudices were concerned, she had, like all other women, sympathy with those kinds of suffering which by experience she understood. Mental distress was beyond her, but for the solace of another's pain she would even have endured a portion herself. When therefore, she heard Helen's story, how her brother had come to her window, that he was ill with brain-fever, as she thought, and talked wildly, she quite approved of her having put him to bed in her own room, and would have got up to help in nursing him. But Helen persuaded her to have her night's rest, and begged her to join with her in warning the servants not to mention his presence in the house, on the ground that it might get abroad that he was out of his mind. They were all old and tolerably faithful, and Leopold had been from childhood such a favourite, that she hoped thus to secure their silence.

"But, child, he must have the doctor," said her aunt.

"Yes, but I will manage him. What a good thing old Mr. Bird is gone! He was such a gossip! We must call in the new doctor, Mr. Faber. I shall see that he understands. He has his practice to make, and will mind what I say."

"Why, child, you are as cunning as an old witch!" said her aunt. "It is very awkward," she went on. "What miserable creatures men are—from first to last! Out of one scrape into another from babies to old men! Would you believe it, my dear?—your uncle, one of the best of men, and most exemplary of clergymen—why, I had to put on his stockings for him every day he got up! Not that my services stopped there either, I can tell you! Latterly I wrote more than half his sermons for him. He never would preach the same sermon twice, you see. He made that a point of honour; and the consequence was that at last he had to come to me. His sermons were nothing the losers, I trust, or our congregation either. I used the same commentaries he did, and you would hardly believe how much I enjoyed the work.—Poor dear boy! we must do what we can for him."

"I will call you if I find it necessary, aunt. I must go to him now, for he cannot bear me out of his sight. Don't please send for the doctor till I see you again."

When she got back to her room, to her great relief she found Leopold asleep. The comfort of the bed after his terrible exhaustion and the hardships he had undergone, had combined with the drug under whose influences he had more or less been ever since first he appeared at Helen's window, and he slept soundly.

But when he woke, he was in a high fever, and Mr. Faber was summoned. He found the state of his patient such that no amount of wild utterance could have surprised him. His brain was burning and his mind all abroad: he tossed from side to side and talked vehemently—but even to Helen unintelligibly.

Mr. Faber had not attended medical classes and walked the hospitals without undergoing the influences of the unbelief prevailing in those regions, where, on the strength of a little knowledge of the human frame, cartloads of puerile ignorance and anile vulgarity, not to mention obscenity, are uttered in the name of truth by men who know nothing whatever of the things that belong to the deeper nature believed in by the devout and simple, and professed also by many who are perhaps yet farther from a knowledge of its affairs than those who thus treat them with contempt. When therefore he came to practise in Glaston, he brought his quota of yeast into the old bottle of that ancient and slumberous town. But as he had to gain for himself a practice, he was prudent enough to make no display of the cherished emptiness of his swept and garnished rooms. I do not mean to blame him. He did not fancy himself the holder of any Mephistophelean commission for the general annihilation of belief like George Bascombe, only one from nature's bureau of ways and means for the cure of the ailing body—which, indeed, to him, comprised all there was of humanity. He had a cold, hard, business-like manner, which, however admirable on some grounds, destroyed any hope Helen had cherished of finding in him one to whom she might disclose her situation.

He proved himself both wise and skilful, yet it was weeks before Leopold began to mend. By the time the fever left him, he was in such a prostrate condition, that it was very doubtful whether yet he could live, and Helen had had to draw largely even upon her fine stock of health.

Her ministration continued most exhausting. Yet now she thought of her life as she had never thought of it before, namely as a thing of worth. It had grown precious to her since it had become the stay of Leopold's. Notwithstanding the terrible state of suspense and horror in which she now lived, seeming to herself at times an actual sharer in her brother's guilt, she would yet occasionally find herself exulting in the thought of being the guardian angel he called her. Now that by his bedside hour plodded after hour in something of sameness and much of weariness, she yet looked back on her past as on the history of a slug.

During all the time she scarcely saw her cousin George, and indeed, she could hardly tell why, shrunk from him. In the cold, bright, shadowless, north-windy day of his presence, there was little consolation to be gathered, and for strength—to face him made a fresh demand upon the little she had. Her physical being had certainly lost. But the countenance which, after a long interval of absence, the curate at length one morning descried in the midst of the congregation, had, along with its pallor and look of hidden and suppressed trouble, gathered the expression of a higher order of existence. Not that she had drawn a single consoling draught from any one of the wells of religion, or now sought the church for the sake of any reminder of something found precious: the great quiet place drew her merely with the offer of its two hours' restful stillness. The thing which had elevated her was simply the fact that, without any thought, not to say knowledge of him, she had yet been doing the will of the Heart of the world. True she had been but following her instinct, and ministering—not to humanity from an enlarged affection, but only to the one being she best loved in the world—a small merit surely!—yet was it the beginning of the way of God, the lovely way, and therefore the face of the maiden had begun to shine with a light which no splendour of physical health, no consciousness of beauty, however just, could have kindled there.

CHAPTER XXX.

THE CURATE'S PROGRESS.

The visits of Wingfold to the little people at the gate not only became frequent, but more and more interesting to him, and as his office occasioned few demands on his attention, Polwarth had plenty of time to give to one who sought instruction in those things which were his very passion. He had never yet had any pupil but his niece, and to find another, and one whose soul was so eager after that of which he had such long-gathered store to dispense, was a keen, pure, and solemn delight. It was that for which he had so often prayed— an outlet for the living waters of his spirit into dry and thirsty lands. He had not much faculty for writing, although now and then he would relieve his heart in verse; and if he had a somewhat remarkable gift of discourse, to attempt public utterance would have been but a vain exposure of his person to vulgar mockery. In Wingfold he had found a man docile and obedient, both thirsting after, and recognizant of the truth, and if he might but aid him in unsealing the well of truth in his own soul, the healing waters might from him flow far and near. Not as the little Zacchæus who pieced his own shortness with the length of the sycamore tree, so to rise above his taller brethren and see Jesus, little Polwarth would lift tall Wingfold on his shoulders, first to see, and then cry aloud to his brethren who was at hand.

For two or three Sundays, the curate, largely assisted by his friend, fed his flock with his gleanings from other men's harvests, and already, though it had not yet come to his knowledge, one consequence was, that complaints, running together, made a pool of discontent, and a semi-public meeting had been held, wherein was discussed, and not finally negatived, the propriety of communicating with the rector on the subject. Some however held that, as the incumbent paid so little attention to his flock, it would be better to appeal to the bishop, and acquaint him with the destitution of that portion of his oversight. But things presently took a new turn, at first surprising, soon alarming to some, and at length, to not a few, appalling.

Obedient to Polwarth's instructions, Wingfold had taken to his New Testament. At first, as he read and sought to understand, ever and anon some small difficulty, notably, foremost of all, the discrepancy in the genealogies— I mention it merely to show the sort of difficulty I mean—would insect-like shoot out of the darkness, and sting him in the face. Some of these he pursued, encountered, crushed—and found he had gained next to nothing by the victory; and Polwarth soon persuaded him to let such, alone for the present, seeing they involved nothing concerning the man at a knowledge of whom it was his business to arrive. But when it came to the perplexity caused by some of the sayings of Jesus himself, it was another matter. He MUST understand these, he thought, or fail to understand the man. Here Polwarth told him that, if, after all, he seemed to fail, he must conclude that possibly the meaning of the words was beyond him, and that the understanding of them depended on a more advanced knowledge of Jesus himself; for, while words reveal the speaker, they must yet lie in the light of something already known of the speaker to be themselves intelligible. Between the mind and the understanding of certain hard utterances, therefore, there must of necessity lie a gradation of easier steps. And here Polwarth was tempted to give him a far more important, because more immediately practical hint, but refrained, from the dread of weakening, by PRESENTATION, the force of a truth which, in DISCOVERY, would have its full effect. For he was confident that the curate, in the temper which was now his, must ere long come immediately upon the truth towards which he was tempted to point him.

On one occasion when Wingfold had asked him whether he saw the meaning of a certain saying of our Lord, Polwarth answered thus:

"I think I do, but whether I could at present make you see it, I cannot tell. I suspect it is one of those concerning which I have already said that you have yet to understand Jesus better before you can understand them. Let me, just to make the nature of what I state clearer to you, ask you one question: tell me, if you can, what, primarily, did Jesus, from his own account of himself, come into the world to do?"

"To save it," answered Wingfold.

"I think you are wrong," returned Polwarth. "Mind I said PRIMARILY. You will yourself come to the same conclusion by and by. Either our Lord was a phantom—a heresy of potent working in the minds of many who would be fierce in its repudiation—or he was a very man, uttering the heart of his life that it might become the life of his brethren; and if so, an honest man can never ultimately fail of getting at what he means. I have seen him described somewhere as a man dominated by the passion of humanity—or something like that. The description does not, to my mind, even shadow the truth. Another passion, if such I may dare to call it, was the light of his life, dominating even that which would yet have been enough to make him lay down his life."

Wingfold went away pondering.

Though Polwarth read little concerning religion except the New Testament, he could yet have directed Wingfold to several books which might have lent him good aid in his quest after the real likeness of the man he sought; but he greatly desired that on the soul of his friend the dawn should break over the mountains of Judæa—the light, I mean, flow from the words themselves of the Son of Man. Sometimes he grew so excited about his pupil and his progress, and looked so anxiously for the news of light in his darkness, that he could not rest at home, but would be out all day in the park—praying, his niece believed, for the young parson. And little did Wingfold suspect that, now and again when his lamp was burning far into the night because he struggled with some hard saying, the little man was going round and round the house, like one muttering charms, only they were prayers for his friend: ill satisfied with his own feeble affection, he would supplement it with its origin, would lay hold upon the riches of the Godhead, crying for his friend to "the first stock-father of gentleness;"—folly all, and fair subject of laughter to such as George Bascombe, if there be no God; but as Polwarth, with his whole, healthy, holy soul believed there is a God—it was for him but simple common sense.

Still no daybreak—and now the miracles had grown troublesome! Could Mr. Polwarth honestly say that he found no difficulty in believing things so altogether out of the common order of events, and so buried in the darkness and dust of antiquity that investigation was impossible?

Mr. Polwarth could not say that he had found no such difficulty.

"Then why should the weight of the story," said Wingfold, "the weight of its proof, I mean, to minds like ours, coming so long after, and by their education incapacitated for believing in such things, in a time when the law of everything is searched into—-"

"And as yet very likely as far from understood as ever," interposed but not interrupted Polwarth.

"Why should the weight of its proof, I ask, be laid upon such improbable things as miracles? That they are necessarily improbable, I presume you will admit."

"Having premised that I believe every one recorded," said Polwarth, "I heartily admit their improbability. But the WEIGHT of proof is not, and never was laid upon them. Our Lord did not make much of them, and did them far more for the individual concerned than for the sake of the beholders. I will not however talk to you about them now. I will merely say that it is not through the miracles you will find the Lord, though, having found him, you will find him there also. The question for you is not, Are the miracles true? but, Was Jesus true? Again I say, you must find him—the man himself. When you have found him, I may perhaps retort upon you the question—Can you believe such improbable things as the miracles, Mr. Wingfold?"

The little man showed pretty plainly by the set of his lips that he meant to say no more, and again Wingfold had, with considerable dissatisfaction and no answer, to go back to his New Testament.

CHAPTER XXXI.

THE CURATE MAKES A DISCOVERY.

At length, one day, as he was working with a harmony, comparing certain passages between themselves, and as variedly given in the gospels, he fell into a half-thinking, half-dreaming mood, in which his eyes, for some time unconsciously, rested on the verse, "Ye will not come unto me that ye might have life:" it mingled itself with his brooding, and by and by, though yet he was brooding rather than meditating, the form of Jesus had gathered, in the stillness of his mental quiescence, so much of reality that at length he found himself thinking of him as of a true-hearted man, mightily in earnest to help his fellows, who could not get them to mind what he told them.

"Ah!" said the curate to himself, "if I had but seen him, would not I have minded him!—would I not have haunted his steps, with question upon question, until I got at the truth!"

Again the more definite thought vanished in the seething chaos of reverie, which dured unbroken for a time,—until again suddenly rose from memory to consciousness and attention the words: "Why call ye me Lord, Lord, and do not the things which I say?"

"Good God!" he exclaimed, "here am I bothering over words, and questioning about this and that, as if I were testing his fitness for a post I had to offer him, and he all the time claiming my obedience! I cannot even, on the spur of the moment at least, tell one thing he wants me to do; and as to doing anything because he told me—not once did I ever! But then how am I to obey him until I am sure of his right to command? I just want to know whether I am to call him Lord or not. No, that won't do either, for he says, Why even of yourselves judge ye not what is right? And do I not know— have I ever even doubted that what he said we ought to do was the right thing to do? Yet here have I, all these years, been calling myself a Christian, ministering, forsooth, in the temple of Christ, as if he were a heathen divinity, who cared for songs and prayers and sacrifices, and cannot honestly say I ever once in my life did a thing because he said so, although the record is full of his earnest, even pleading words! I have NOT been an honest man, and how should a dishonest man be a judge over that man who said he was the Christ of God? Would it be any wonder if the things he uttered should be too high and noble to be by such a man recognized as truth?"

With this, yet another saying dawned upon, him: IF ANY MAN WILL DO HIS WILL, HE SHALL KNOW OF THE DOCTRINE, WHETHER IT BE OF GOD, OR
WHETHER I SPEAK OF MYSELF.

He went into his closet and shut to the door—came out again, and went straight to visit a certain grievous old woman.

The next open result was, that, on the following Sunday, a man went up into the pulpit who, for the first time in his life, believed he had something to say to his fellow-sinners. It was not now the sacred spoil of the best of gleaning or catering that he bore thither with him, but the message given him by a light in his own inward parts, discovering therein the darkness and the wrong.

He opened no sermon-case, nor read words from any book, save, with trembling voice, these:

"WHY CALL YE ME LORD, LORD, AND DO NOT THE THINGS WHICH I SAY?"

I pause for a moment in my narrative to request the sympathy of such readers as may be capable of affording it, for a man whose honesty makes him appear egotistic. When a man, finding himself in a false position, is yet anxious to do the duties of that position until such time as, if he should not in the meantime have verified it, and become able to fill it with honesty, he may honourably leave it, I think he may well be pardoned if, of inward necessity, he should refer to himself in a place where such reference may be either the greatest impiety, or the outcome of the truest devotion. In him it was neither: it was honesty—and absorption in the startled gaze of a love that believed it had caught a glimmer of the passing garment of the Truth. Thus strengthened—might I not say inspired? for what is the love of truth and the joy therein, if not a breathing into the soul of the breath of life from the God of truth?—he looked round upon his congregation as he had never dared until now—saw face after face, and knew it—saw amongst the rest that of Helen Lingard, so sadly yet not pitifully altered, with a doubt if it could be she; trembled a little with a new excitement, which one less modest or less wise might have taken—how foolishly!—instead of the truth perceived, for the inspiration of the spirit; and, sternly suppressing the emotion, said,

"My hearers, I come before you this morning to utter the first word of truth it has ever been given to ME to utter."

His hearers stared both mentally and corporeally.

"Is he going to deny the Bible?" said some.

—"It will be the last," said others, "if the rector hear in time how you have been disgracing yourself and profaning his pulpit."

"And," the curate went on, "it would be as a fire in my bones did I attempt to keep it back.

"In my room, three days ago, I was reading the strange story of the man who appeared in Palestine saying that he was the Son of God, and came upon those words of his which I have now read in your hearing. At their sound the accuser, Conscience, awoke in my bosom, and asked, 'Doest thou the things he saith to thee?' And I thought with myself,—'Have I this day done anything he says to me?—when did I do anything I had heard of him? Did I ever'— to this it came at last—'Did I ever, in all my life, do one thing because he said to me DO THIS?' And the answer was NO, NEVER. Yet there I was, not only calling myself a Christian, but on the strength of my Christianity, it was to be presumed, living amongst you, and received by you, as your helper on the way to the heavenly kingdom—a living falsehood, walking and talking amongst you!"

"What a wretch!" said one man to himself, who made a large part of his living by the sale of under-garments whose every stitch was an untacking of the body from the soul of a seamstress. "Bah!" said some. "A hypocrite, by his own confession!" said others. "Exceedingly improper!" said Mrs. Ramshorn. "Unheard-of and most unclerical behaviour! And actually to confess such paganism!" For Helen, she waked up a little, began to listen, and wondered what he had been saying that a wind seemed to have blown rustling among the heads of the congregation.

"Having made this confession," Wingfold proceeded, "you will understand that whatever I now say, I say to and of myself as much as to and of any other to whom it may apply."

He then proceeded to show that faith and obedience are one and the same spirit, passing as it were from room to room in the same heart: what in the heart we call faith, in the will we call obedience. He showed that the Lord refused absolutely the faith that found its vent at the lips in the worshipping words, and not at the limbs in obedient action—which some present pronounced bad theology, while others said to themselves surely that at least was common sense. For Helen, what she heard might be interesting to clergymen, or people like her aunt who had to do with such matters, but to her it was less than nothing and vanity, whose brother lay at home "sick in heart and sick in head."

But hard thoughts of him could not stay the fountain of Wingfold's utterance, which filled as it flowed. Eager after a right presentation of what truth he saw, he dwelt on the mockery it would be of any man to call him the wisest, the best, the kindest, yea and the dearest of men, yet never heed either the smallest request or the most urgent entreaty he made.

"A Socinian!" said Mrs. Ramshorn.

"There's stuff in the fellow!" said the rector's churchwarden, who had been brought up a Wesleyan.

"He'd make a fellow fancy he did believe all his grandmother told him!" thought Bascombe.

As he went on, the awakened curate grew almost eloquent. His face shone with earnestness. Even Helen found her gaze fixed upon him, though she had not a notion what he was talking about. He closed at length with these words:

"After the confession I have now made to you, a confession which I have also entreated everyone to whom it belongs to make to himself and his God, it follows that I dare not call myself a Christian. How should such a one as I know anything about that which, if it be true at all, is the loftiest, the one all-absorbing truth in the universe? How should such a fellow as I"—he went on, growing scornful at himself in the presence of the truth—"judge of its sacred probabilities? or, having led such a life of simony, be heard when he declares that such a pretended message from God to men seems too good to be true? The things therein contained I declare good, yet went not and did them. Therefore am I altogether out of court, and must not be heard in the matter.

"No, my hearers, I call not myself a Christian, but I call everyone here who obeys the word of Jesus, who restrains anger, who declines judgment, who practises generosity, who loves his enemies, who prays for his slanderers, to witness my vow, that I will henceforth try to obey him, in the hope that he whom he called God and his Father, will reveal to him whom you call your Lord Jesus Christ, that into my darkness I may receive the light of the world!"

"A professed infidel!" said Mrs. Ramshorn. "A clever one too! That was a fine trap he laid for us, to prove us all atheists as well as himself! As if any mere mortal COULD obey the instructions of the Saviour! He was divine; we are but human!"

She might have added, "And but poor creatures as such," but did not go so far, believing herself more than an average specimen.

But there was one shining face which, like a rising sun of love and light and truth, "pillowed his chin," not "on an orient wave," but on the book-board of a free seat. The eyes of it were full of tears, and the heart behind it was giving that God and Father thanks, for this was more, far more than he had even hoped for, save in the indefinite future. The light was no longer present as warmth or vivification alone, but had begun to shine as light in the heart of his friend, to whom now, praised be God! the way lay open into all truth. And when the words came, in a voice that once more trembled with emotion—"Now to God the Father,"—he bent down his face, and the poor, stunted, distorted frame and great grey head were grievously shaken with the sobs of a mighty gladness. Truth in the inward parts looked out upon him from the face of one who stood before the people their self-denied teacher! How would they receive it? It mattered not. Those whom the Father had drawn, would hear.

Polwarth neither sought the curate in the vestry, waited for him at the church-door, nor followed him to his lodging. He was not of those who compliment a man on his fine sermon. How grandly careless are some men of the risk of ruin their praises are to their friends! "Let God praise him!" said Polwarth; "I will only dare to love him." He would not toy with his friend's waking Psyche.

CHAPTER XXXII.

HOPES.

It was the first Sunday Helen had gone to church since her brother came to her. On the previous Sunday he had passed some crisis and begun to improve, and by the end of the week was so quiet, that longing for a change of atmosphere, and believing he might be left with the housekeeper, she had gone to church. On her return she heard he was no worse, although he had "been a-frettin' after her." She hurried to him as if he had been her baby.

"What do you go to church for?" he asked, half-petulantly, like a spoilt child, with languid eyes whence the hard fire had vanished. "What's the use of it?"

He looked at her, waiting an answer.

"Not much," replied Helen. "I like the quiet and the music. That's all."

He seemed disappointed, and lay still for a few moments.

"In old times," he said at last, "the churches used to be a refuge: I suppose that is why one can't help feeling as if some safety were to be got from them yet.—Was your cousin George there this morning?"

"Yes, he went with us," answered Helen.

"I should like to see him. I want somebody to talk to."

Helen was silent. She was more occupied however in answering to herself the question why she shrank so decidedly from bringing Bascombe into the sick-room, than in thinking what she should say to Leopold. The truth was the truth, and why should she object to Leopold's knowing, or at least being told as well as herself, that he need fear no punishment in the next world, whatever he might have to encounter in this; that there was no frightful God who hated wrong-doing to be terrified at; that even the badness of his own action need not distress him, for he and it would pass away as the blood he had shed had already vanished from the earth? Ought it not to encourage the poor fellow?—But to what? To live on and endure his misery, or to put an end to it and himself at once? Or perhaps to plunge into vice that he might escape the consciousness of guilt and the dread of the law?

I will not say that exactly such a train of thought as this passed through her mind, but of whatever sort it was, it brought her no nearer to a desire for the light of George Bascombe's presence by the bedside of her guilty brother. At the same time her partiality for her cousin made her justify his exclusion thus: "George is so good himself, he is only fit for the company of good people. He would not in the least understand my poor Poldie, and would be too hard upon him."

Since her brother's appearance, in fact, she had seen very little of her cousin, and this not merely because her presence was so much required in the sick-chamber, but because she was herself unwilling to meet him. She had felt, almost without knowing it, that his character was unsympathetic, and that his loud, cold good-nature could never recognise or justify such love as she bore to her brother! Nor was this all; for, remembering how he had upon one occasion expressed himself with regard to criminals, she feared even to look in his face, lest his keen, questioning, unsparing eye should read in her soul that she was the sister of a murderer.

Before this time however a hint of light had appeared in the clouds that enwrapped her and Leopold: she had begun to doubt whether he had really committed the crime of which he accused himself. There had been no inquiry after him, except from his uncle, concerning his absence from Cambridge, for which his sudden attack of brain fever served as more than sufficient excuse. That there had been such a murder, the newspapers left her no room to question—but might not the relation in which he stood to the victim— the horror of her death, the insidious approaches of the fever, and the influences of that hateful drug, have combined to call up an hallucination of blood-guiltiness? And what at length all but satisfied her of the truth of her conjecture was that, when he began to recover, Leopold seemed himself in doubt at times whether his sense of guilt had not its origin in some one or other of the many dreams which had haunted him throughout his illness, knowing only too well that it was long since dreams had become to him more real than the greater part of what was going on around him. To this blurring and confusing of consciousness it probably contributed, that, in the first stages of the fever, he was under the influence of the same drug which had been working upon his brain up to the very moment when he committed the crime.

During the week the hope had almost settled into conviction; and one consequence was that, although she was not a whit more inclined to introduce George Bascombe to the sick-chamber, she found herself not only equal, but no longer averse to meeting him; and on the following Saturday, when he presented himself as usual, come to spend the Sunday, she listened to her aunt, and consented to go out with him for a ride—in the evening, however, when Mrs. Rainshorn herself, who had shown Leopold great and genuine kindness, would be able to sit with him. They therefore had dinner early, and Helen went again to her brother's room, unwilling to leave him a moment until she gave up her charge to her aunt.

They had tea together, and Leopold was very quiet. It is wonderful with what success the mind will accommodate itself, in its effort after peace, to the presence of the most torturing thought. But Helen took this quietness for a sign of innocence, not knowing that the state of the feelings is neither test nor gauge of guilt. The nearer perfection a character is, the louder is the cry of conscience at the appearance of fault; and, on the other hand, the worst criminals have had the easiest minds.

Helen also was quiet, and fell into a dreamy mood, watching her brother, who every now and then turned on her a look of love and gratitude which moved her heart to its very depths. Not until she heard the horses coming round from the stable, did she rise to go and change her dress.

"I shall not be long away from you, Poldie," she said.

"Do not forget me, Helen," he returned. "If you forget me, an enemy will think of me."

His love comforted her, and yet further strengthened her faith in his innocence; and it was with a kind of half-repose, timid, wavering, and glad, upon her countenance—how different from the old, dull, wooden quiescence!—that she joined her cousin in the hall. A moment, and he had lifted her to the saddle, and was mounted by her side.

CHAPTER XXXIII.

THE RIDE.

A soft west wind, issuing as from the heart of a golden vase filled with roses, met them the instant they turned out of the street, walking their horses towards the park-gate.

Something—was it in the evening, or was it in his own soul?—had prevailed to the momentary silencing of George Bascombe:—it may have been but the influence of the cigar which Helen had begged him to finish. Helen too was silent: she felt as if the low red sun, straight into which they seemed to be riding, blotted out her being in the level torrent of his usurping radiance. Neither of them spoke a word until they had passed through the gate into the park.

It was a perfect English summer evening—warm, but not sultry. As they walked their horses up the carriage way, the sun went down, and as if he had fallen like a live coal into some celestial magazine of colour and glow, straightway blazed up a slow explosion of crimson and green in a golden triumph—pure fire, the smoke and fuel gone, and the radiance alone left. And now Helen received the second lesson of her initiation into the life of nature: she became aware that the whole evening was thinking around her, and as the dusk grew deeper and the night grew closer, the world seemed to have grown dark with its thinking. Of late Helen had been driven herself to think—if not deeply, yet intensely—and so knew what it was like, and felt at home with the twilight.

They turned from the drive on to the turf. Their horses tossed up their heads, and set off, unchecked, at a good pelting gallop, across the open park. On Helen's cheek the wind blew cooling, strong, and kind. As if flowing from some fountain above, in an unseen unbanked river, down through the stiller ocean of the air, it seemed to bring to her a vague promise, almost a precognition, of peace—which, however, only set her longing after something—she knew not what—something of which she only knew that it would fill the longing the wind had brought her. The longing grew and extended—went stretching on and on into an infinite of rest. And as they still galloped, and the light-maddened colours sank into smoky peach, and yellow green, and blue gray, the something swelled and swelled in her soul, and pulled and pulled at her heart, until the tears were running down her face: for fear Bascombe should see them, she gave her horse the rein, and fled from him into the friendly dusk that seemed to grade time into eternity.

Suddenly she found herself close to a clump of trees, which overhung the deserted house. She had made a great circuit without knowing it. A pang shot to her heart, and her tears ceased to flow. The night, silent with thought, held THAT also in its bosom! She drew rein, turned, and waited for Bascombe.

"What a chase you've given me, Helen!" he cried, while yet pounding away some score of yards off.

"A wild-goose one you mean, cousin?"

"It would have been if I had thought to catch you on this ancient cocktail."

"Don't abuse the old horse, George: he has seen better days. I would gladly have mounted you more to your mind, but you know I could not—except indeed I had given you my Fanny, and taken the old horse myself. I have ridden him."

"The lady ought always to be the better mounted," returned George coolly. "For my part, I much prefer it, because then I need not be anxious about whether I am boring her or not: if I am, she can run away."

"You cannot suppose I thought you a bore to-night. A more sweetly silent gentleman none could wish for squire."

"Then it was my silence bored you.—Shall I tell you what I was thinking about?"

"If you like. I was thinking how pleasant it would be to ride on and on into eternity," said Helen.

"That feeling of continuity," returned George, "is a proof of the painlessness of departure. No one can ever know when he ceases to be, because then he is not; and that is how some men come to fancy they feel as if they were going to live for ever. But the worst of it is that they no sooner fancy it, than it seems to them a probable as well as delightful thing to go on and on and never cease. This comes of the man's having no consciousness of ceasing, and when one is comfortable, it always seems good to go on. A child is never willing to turn from the dish of which he is eating to another. It is more he wants, not another."

"That is if he likes it," said Helen.

"Everybody likes it," said George, "—more or less."

"I am not so sure of EVERYbody," replied Helen. "Do you imagine that twisted little dwarf-woman that opened the gate for us is content with her lot?"

"No, that is impossible—while she sees you and remains what she is. But I said nothing of contentment. I was but thinking of the fools who, whether content or not, yet want to live for ever, and so, very conveniently, take their longing for immortality, which they call an idea innate in the human heart, for a proof that immortality is their rightful inheritance."

"How then do you account for the existence and universality of the idea?" asked Helen, who had happened lately to come upon some arguments on the other side.

But while she spoke thus indifferently she felt in her heart like one who wakes from a delicious swim in the fairest of rivers, to find that the clothes have slipped from the bed to the floor:—that was all his river and all his swim!

"I account for its existence as I have just said; and for its universality by denying it. It is NOT universal, for *I* haven't it."

"At least you will not deny that men, even when miserable, shrink from dying?"

"Anything, everything is unpleasant out of its due time. I will allow, for the sake of argument, that the thought of dying is always unpleasant. But wherefore so? Because, in the very act of thinking it, the idea must always be taken from the time that suits with it—namely, its own time, when it will at length, and ought at length to come—and placed in the midst of the lively present, with which assuredly it does not suit. To life, death must be always hateful. In the rush and turmoil of effort, how distasteful even the cave of the hermit—let ever such a splendid view spread abroad before its mouth! But when it comes it will be pleasant enough, for then its time will have come also—the man will be prepared for it by decay and cessation. If one were to tell me that he had that endless longing for immortality, of which hitherto I have only heard at second hand, I would explain it to him thus:—Your life, I would say, not being yet complete, still growing, feels in itself the onward impulse of growth, and, unable to think of itself as other than complete, interprets that onward impulse as belonging to the time around it instead of the nature within it. Or rather let me say, the man feels in himself the elements of more, and not being able to grasp the notion of his own completeness, which is so far from him, transposes the feeling of growth and sets it beyond himself, translating it at the same time into an instinct of duration, a longing after what he calls eternal life. But when the man is complete, then comes decay and brings its own contentment with it—as will also death, when it arrives in its own proper season of fulness and ripeness."

Helen said nothing in reply. She thought her cousin very clever, but could not enjoy what he said—not in the face of that sky, and in the yet lingering reflection of the feelings it had waked in her. He might be right, but now at least she wanted no more of it. She even felt as if she would rather cherish a sweet deception for the comfort of the moment in which the weaver's shuttle flew, than take to her bosom a cold killing fact.

Such were indeed an unworthy feeling to follow! Of all things let us have the truth—even of fact! But to deny what we cannot prove, not even casts into our ice-house a spadeful of snow. What if the warm hope denied should be the truth after all? What if it was the truth in it that drew the soul towards it by its indwelling reality, and its relations with her being, even while she took blame for suffering herself to be enticed by a sweet deception? Alas indeed for men if the life and the truth are not one, but fight against each other! Surely it says something for the divine nature of him that denies the divine, when he yet cleaves to what he thinks the truth, although it denies the life, and blots the way to the better from every chart!

"And what were you thinking of, George?" said Helen, willing to change the subject.

"I was thinking," he answered, "let me see!—oh! yes—I was thinking of that very singular case of murder. You must have seen it in the newspapers. I have long had a doubt whether I were better fitted for a barrister or a detective. I can't keep my mind off a puzzling case.—You must have heard of this one— the girl they found lying in her ball-dress in the middle of a wood—stabbed to the heart?"

"I do remember something of it," answered Helen, gathering a little courage to put into her voice from the fact that her cousin could hardly see her face. "Then the murderer has not been discovered?"

"That is the point of interest. Not a trace of him! Not a soul suspected even!"

Helen drew a deep breath.

"Had it been in Rome, now," George went on. "But in a quiet country place in England! The thing seems incredible! So artistically done!—no struggle!— just one blow right to the heart, and the assassin gone as if by magic!—no weapon dropped!—nothing to give a clue! The whole thing suggests a practised hand.—But why such a one for the victim? Had it been some false member of a secret society thus immolated, one could understand it. But a merry girl at a ball!—it IS strange! I SHOULD like to try the unravelling of it."

"Has nothing then been done?" said Helen with a gasp, to hide which she moved in her saddle, as if readjusting her habit.

"Oh, everything—of course. There was instant pursuit on the discovery of the body, but they seem to have got on the track of the wrong man—or, indeed, for anything certain, of no man at all. A coast-guardsman says that, on the night or rather morning in question, he was approaching a little cove on the shore, not above a mile from the scene of the tragedy, with an eye upon what seemed to be two fishermen preparing to launch their boat, when he saw a third man come running down the steep slope from the pastures above, and jump into the stern of it. Ere he could reach the spot, they were off, and had hoisted two lugsails. The moon was in the first of her last quarter, and gave light enough for what he reported. But, when inquiries founded on this evidence were made, nothing whatever could be discovered concerning boat or men. The next morning no fishing-boat was lacking, and no fisherman would confess to having gone from that cove. The marks of the boat's keel, and of the men's feet, on the sand, if ever there were any, had been washed out by the tide. It was concluded that the thing had been pre-arranged and provided for, and that the murderer had escaped, probably to Holland. Thereupon telegrams were shot in all directions, but no news could be gathered of any suspicious landing on the opposite coast. There the matter rests, or at least has rested for many weeks. Neither parents, relatives, nor friends appear to have a suspicion of anyone."

"Are there no conjectures as to motives?" asked Helen, feeling with joy her power of dissimulation gather strength.

"No end of them. She was a beautiful creature, they say, sweet-tempered as a dove, and of course fond of admiration—whence the conjectures all turn on jealousy. The most likely thing seems, that she had some squire of low degree, of whom neither parents nor friends knew anything. That they themselves suspect this, appears likely from their more than apathy with regard to the discovery of the villain. I am strongly inclined to take the matter in hand myself."

"We must get him out of the country as soon as possible," thought Helen.

"I should hardly have thought it worthy of your gifts, George," she said, "to turn police-man. For my part, I should not relish hunting down any poor wretch."

"The sacrifice of individual choice is a claim society has upon each of its members," returned Bascombe. "Every murderer hanged, or better, imprisoned for life, is a gain to the community."

Helen said no more, and presently turned homewards, on the plea that she must not be longer absent from her invalid.

END OF THE FIRST VOLUME.